GW00393854

CHAPTER 1.

There are two main lies regarding travelling, especially in Asia, that are bounded about with a complete disregard for any poor soul that gets suckered into believing them. The first one, thinking about it in depth is not so much a lie as it is a misconception. The people spilling it to anyone who will listen aren't being malicious. They are just using an old cliché of what suddenly being fucking hot and uncomfortable feels like.

First lie. 'It's like walking into a wall of heat.' It isn't. Walking into a wall of heat would be the equivalent of stepping into a furnace. Most of us have heard of or seen water boarding in a film by now. Thanks to the US war on terror almost everyone has come across a story of a terrorist being whisked away to a black site to experience this very strange way of washing. Stepping off a plane in Asia in the middle of their high season having just come from a relatively cold climate is like being waterboarded with a hot towel across your face while having warm water poured down your pants.

During my flight to Thailand, I had the unfortunate experience of being sat next to an overweight "seasoned" traveller who delighted in telling me how many times he had been to Thailand.

'I'm telling you Ruben, it's like walking into a wall of heat like you can't imagine.'

'Right.' I said. 'And what do you recommend to get through it?' I didn't care what his thoughts were but after seven hours trying to ignore him and nothing else to do, I gave into his incessant talking. It had become futile to resist.

No one told me of the boredom that comes with a long-haul flight. And this is where the second lie kicks in. This one I think is used in a malicious way. Read any travel book, watch a programme with a preening overpaid celebrity being ushered around a picturesque island and it'll be spouted out. I would come to understand the lie more in the not too distant future but at this moment in time I knew enough of travelling to know that getting from point A to point X is not the best bit about travelling. It was quite possibly the worst part. I wasn't sure how much more I could take. I started to wish I had brought some pills with me. A few diazepam, maybe even a light beta-blocker would do around now. I looked over to Charlottes seat. She was sleeping. Three hours and she hadn't moved. Had to have taken something. I was jealous. The thought of waking her popped into my head. It would seem a bit sexual predator though, so I pushed the idea away.

'So, that's all the help and advice I can offer to be fair.'

I looked at his chubby face. Not a word of what he had been so pleased about had entered my brain. If all backpackers were like him, I would be home in a week. I needed to relax.

'I'm gonna take a piss. Excuse me.'

'Um, yeah sure. Can I get you a drink?'

'I'll take a whiskey if you're going please.'

I watched him press the steward button above his head. His arm fat wobbling as he stretched up and then turned in the direction of the toilet. I would have to ask his name when I returned. I had Mark in my head. Or could have been Martin.

Looking at the no smoking signs it dawned on me that this was the longest I had gone without lighting up in years. It felt nice, like I had achieved something. I flushed, washed my hands, and slid the bi-folding doors open. Heading back to my seat I had a sudden onset of a feeling that was almost alien to me. An enormous sense of calm washed over me filling my entire being. The interior of the plane was dark with just the glow from the back of seat TV's, giving off just enough light to guide you but not enough to disturb your sleep. Matched with the gentle humming of the air-conditioning and rumble of the jet engines it was there in front of me how people could sleep for half the length of a continent. I just needed to take a minute to see it.

Getting closer to my row I noticed two very delicate arms dancing in the air. They didn't belong to my portly travel companion. I glanced across to where Charlotte had been unconscious.

'Welcome back. I hope you don't mind me crashing your boy's trip. Bernie said it would be ok for me to sit down.'

'Bernie?'

'Yeah. He's just gone to the toilet. He said you had a spare seat between you.'

I definitely didn't mind Charlotte sitting next to me. Not only could she act as a buffer, but she was funny. Genuinely funny, I didn't laugh at her jokes because she was so hot but because they were actually hilarious.

'Why would I mind. Have you spoken to him? He's a bit fucking weird.'

She laughed. 'No weirder than you to be fair.'

Moving to the middle seat I slid down into mine. I noticed she had drunk some of the drink the steward had kindly brought for me. I was slightly annoyed. 'Did you want to finish this, and I'll get another?' I said.

'It's fine.' She replied pulling a bottle of water from somewhere hidden. 'Not a huge lover of whiskey.'

I sipped from the glass and tried to think of something to say.

'So why do you think Bernie is weird? He seemed fine to me.'

'How do you know his name is Bernie? I'm sure it's Mark or

Martin. It definitely begins with an M.'

She flicked through the channels, dismissing films and TV programmes without giving them a second chance. 'I asked him. You've sat next to him for the last seven odd hours. She sipped her water while mockingly shaking her head. 'How do you not know?'

'Anything you've seen on here? I'm not a lover of the TV to be honest.' I said.

'Why's that?'

'Stops people taking in their surroundings and what's happening in the world.'

She pushed herself up on her elbows and looked around the lifeless plane. I wished I hadn't tried to be thought provoking and a smart arse.

'Obviously, I don't mean right now. In general, I don't like TV's.' She didn't reply this time.

I watched as Bernie's chubby face made its way back to us. He was clutching some packets in each hand.

'He's not a bad person you know. You need to give people a chance.'

I looked at her. Her brown eyes were captivating. I wanted to hold her hand.

'I managed to snag some crispies.'

Bad person or not I wanted to slap him for saying "crispies".

'Yummy.' I said standing and letting him squeeze past. He managed to turn mid-way, so he almost pressed his penis into Charlottes face. The look on his face gave away that that was the closest his dick had ever come to another humans, mouth. I gagged. He slouched down in his seat and threw the bags of peanuts and crisps around.

'I said to Charlotte, she's more than welcome to sit with us as long as the flight crew allow her to.' He began to do a strange dance with his fingers while deciding which crisp to eat first.

I nodded not really listening but enjoying the dry roasted peanuts. These times would come to an abrupt end on flights soon. It would become apparent in a few years that it is not a good idea to have people eating nuts in an enclosed space where you could potentially have someone who's head would explode at a mere whiff of a packet of KP's.

'Did you get the whiskey, Ruben?'

'I did, thank you. Looks like someone had taken a large swig before I got back though.'

He didn't hear. He had already turned his attention to a film that had caught his eye. Charlotte leaned across and very gently stroked the back of my hand.

'Leave him to watch the film Ruben. He's incredibly nervous.'

'What makes you say that? He's been to Thailand dozens of times. When we have spoken that's all he's talked about. I thought I was going to have to tell him to shut up.'

'I asked him a few things about Bangkok, and it was like he was reciting memorised passages from the book.'

'The Bible?'

'Don't be an arse, Ruben you know what I'm talking about.'

'Just call it Lonely Planet then.'

I looked across at Bernie, he had jammed in some ear pods and was shovelling mini cheddars while sipping his Heineken. He didn't appear nervous. I was nervous. Not about being in a country I knew nothing about but more about the loneliness and what that can bring.

'Ruben.'

'Yes.'

'Stop staring. Where did you go?'

She hadn't moved her hand from my wrist, so I gently slid my arm away and made a grab for my drink. It was clumsily done. She noticed, how could she not, her own hands went back to her lap.

'Are you not nervous?'

'About what? I've been dreaming of this for years.'

'What about if you get ill? Or when you can't find anywhere to stay?'

'I haven't really thought...'

I cut her off. 'Shit, what about if you get so ill that you're stuck inside an awful fucking hell hole shitting yourself to death and nobody finds your body until the maid comes to change your towels.'

She stroked the side of my face and took the whiskey from my clammy hand. I was sweating. A cold sweat. The type you get when you realise you've made a huge fucking mistake and you are flying towards an essentially third world country with no idea of what you're supposed to do when you get there.

'Take a deep breath Ruben.'

I wasn't sure if it was me, but the plane was getting darker. I couldn't work out if someone was turning the lights down further. My brain felt like it was going to explode through my ears. There was an immense pressure building inside my head.

'Ruben, listen to my voice. It's OK to be a little concerned or even worried. It's natural. I'm sure many people have had a panic attack when they realise that they aren't going to a Sandals resort.' She pushed the hair away from my face. The way Charlie would have. I started to calm down. 'But you will have to stop being a little girl.' She started laughing.

I looked passed her at Bernie. He was chuckling away. His cheeks were wobbling.

'Why are you laughing?'

'I thought I was the only one shitting myself.'

I looked back to Charlotte. She was smiling. I felt sick. Snatching back the whiskey I drained the glass.

'Seriously Ruben, where the fuck are you staying that you're expecting maids to find your lifeless shit-stained body?'

I didn't answer. For the first time on this flight, I needed a cigarette. Pushing the call button, I caught Bernie's attention. He was trying to ram his earphones back into his big ears.

'Yeah?' He said.

'Why are you shitting yourself? I thought you had been there dozens of times?'

'Why did you think that?'

'Because you fucking said so.'

'Shit, sorry Ruben. I've never really been there before. I do know a few people that have, and they all speak fondly of the place.'

'But you definitely fucking said you had been there. It's a bit of a weird thing to do, don't you think.'

'OK Ruben, I think that will do.' Charlotte said.

Looking from Charlotte to Bernie I realised I may have raised my voice and been a bit too aggressive in my outburst. Bernie seemed on the verge of tears and Charlotte looked uncomfortable by the whole situation.

'I'm sorry.' I said. 'But you did make out that it had been you that had travelled through Thailand. You came across as the original intrepid explorer.'

I didn't wait for either of them to answer. Putting my headphones in I pressed the call button again. I really needed a drink now and a cigarette. The calm had gone and had been replaced by sheer anxiety. I wanted to go home. Fuck Thailand and fuck travelling. I tried to focus on the seat back screen. Altitude was forty-nine thousand feet, ground speed, five hundred miles an hour. I hated these things.

CHAPTER 2.

'Have you finished having your little melt down?'

I was stood outside the toilet. Charlotte had returned to her seat not long after my outburst. Bernie still hadn't looked at me let alone spoken to me. To be honest I didn't care too much if he never acknowledged me again. I had every intention of leaving him at the airport anyway. Charlotte on the other hand was different. I wanted to throw my arms around her at every opportunity and not let go. I'd only known her for the briefest of times, thirteen hours to be precise. She didn't seem to be someone to suffer any of my shit. I knew I would fuck it up eventually, but I hoped it would take longer than usual. And hopefully longer than half a day.

'Yeah, shit. I'm sorry about that. I don't know what came over me.'

'Have you apologised to Bernie yet?'

'No why? He fucking lied.'

'Child.' She smiled. 'Anyway, how much longer are you going to hang around here trying to steal bottles of whiskey?'

'What? I'm waiting for the toilet.'

'Fuck off Ruben. I've seen you grab at least three bottles already. The drinks are free for Christs sake.'

'Yes, but they limit you and only give out one little bottle at a time. And don't take the Lords name in vain.'

'Then you should have brought some of your own.'

She grabbed my arm and kissed me. I pulled her closer and made a fumbled grab for her arse. She stopped kissing me and smiled again. I loved her lips. They are close to perfect. Not too big to look fake but big enough to make it feel like you were being kissed by pillows. Her teeth were amazing too. Trying to put into words how she made me feel was almost futile. I couldn't find words that wouldn't sound childlike.

'Not the right place for that I think.'

She stood back against the toilet door.

'I guess.' I said. 'So, have you thought anymore of my offer to stay with me at the hotel I've booked?'

'Yes. My answer is still no. Have you thought about coming down to the Koh San Road and staying with me?'

'Like I said before, I'm not staying in that shit hole.'

She laughed. 'I'm going back to my seat. Happy stealing.'

'I'm not.' I called after her.

I watched as she squeezed between the rows of sleeping bodies. She gently brushed the arms of people as she went. Most people didn't notice her touch. The ones that did she smiled at and I could almost feel them melt the same way I did. I reached around the curtain again and snatched another short. Drinking it down I leant back against the wall and thought of Charlie. I wondered what she was doing, whether she was happy. Hopefully, Scotland was being kind to her. Fucking Scotland. There wasn't much I could do either way.

'Can I help you Sir?' I turned my head in the direction of the voice but didn't answer. My brain wouldn't work. I couldn't get the thought from my mind to my mouth. 'Sir, is everything OK?'

'Yes, sorry.' It finally kicked in. 'God I'm really sorry. I was miles away.'

'That's not a problem sir. How can I help?'

I stared around at the sleeping bodies and the flickering TV screens. I wanted to scream, rip the doors open and jump into the dark night sky. I think we were somewhere over the Indian Ocean. At least I wouldn't die five miles from where I was born.

'Can I grab a few whiskeys and a coke please. I'm having trouble sleeping.'

'Certainly, sir.'

He reached down without a second glance. This was a man who knew his way around a trolly or two.

'I've heard if you down a couple of these with your sleep mask on you'll be asleep in no time.' He gave me the bottles and a subtle wink. 'If not, you come back and see me and I'm sure we can think of a way to relieve your anxiety.'

I downed the first bottle as I sat back down. Looking across to Charlotte she was deeply involved in a book. I couldn't make out the title from where I was sat. I turned to Bernie. He was asleep and dribbling. His mask had slipped slightly and was only half covering one of his eyes. I stared at his red cheeks for a while and moved my gaze down the entire length of his body. I hadn't noticed how white he was before. I could obviously only see the skin on show, but it was very milky. He was close to being an albino. I'd have to check for red eyes when he woke. I hadn't noticed the colour before but doubt I would have missed them.

'He's gonna fucking burn to death.' I said only half to myself.

The old pervy looking man the row in front turned and stared at me then arched his neck to take in the pale blancmange sat next to me. He snorted and went back to his magazine. I took it that he agreed with me.

I reached up and switched my light off and imagined myself back in my little flat in Islington before I meet Charlie and long before I stepped foot on this tin tube. I prayed to which ever fucking God was listening tonight to let me sleep a peaceful sleep. If only a couple of hours. As I opened and drank two tiny bottles, I thought of the old pervert in front trawling the Bangkok bars looking for young boys or girls. Maybe he had a penchant for Ladyboys. Then I started to think of what a Ladyboy looked like. Could you tell they were men? Did they hang out together and have a club like the British Legion? Was it politically correct to even call them Ladyboys anymore? My head started pounding again with all the questions. I pulled my mask down and tried to sleep.

CHAPTER 3.

'Ladies and Gentlemen, we will soon be arriving at Bangkok International Airport.'

I woke with a start almost knocking the last bottle of whiskey off the tray. Bernie was looking at me like a demented idiot.

'Were here Ruben.'

'I gathered that Bernie. How long did I sleep?'

'Fuck knows. Look out of the window. The weather looks amazing. I bet it's hot.'

'It does mate. I'm sure the pilot will tell you how hot in a minute or two.'

I drank the last bottle and glanced over to Charlotte. She smiled and gave me a reassuring, "it'll be ok" thumbs up. I buckled my seat belt and got ready for landing.

'So where are you staying?'

'Haven't decided to be honest. I did speak to Charlotte about sharing a taxi to The Road, so I'll probably take a walk there and find something.'

'The Road? When did this little chat happen?'

'Yeah, the Koh San Road.' He looked at me like I was stupid for not knowing. 'When you were asleep, she came back over. We had a lovely long talk about where we planned to go. She's really nice.'

I was jealous. Charlotte had kissed me not him, but I was jealous of the intimacy having a deep conversation can bring and that she had chosen him to share that with. I felt like it was me muscling in on his friend.

'I know how nice she is. I met her first don't forget.' I was pissed off at his intrusion into my affairs.

'OK Ruben. We just had a chat.'

'Fine. Also stop shortening everything.'

"Ladies and Gentlemen, the crew will be making their way through the cabin to collect any pieces of rubbish before we make our final decent into Bangkok International. The weather is forecast to be a very welcoming thirty-two degrees and we will be landing under a beautiful clear blue sky."

'What do you mean "stop shortening everything".'

'Just call it Koh San Road or the Lonely Planet. It doesn't sound cool or like you live out here because you call it "The Road".' I used my fingers to create air quotes. I immediately hated myself for doing it. 'It just sounds cunty.'

He was taken aback slightly. Cunty is not a word I had ever used before and instantly regretted using it to him. Only partly because it may have offended him but also because saying the word cunty was cunty itself. I did definitely regret being the cause of the look on his face though. He looked like a puppy who had just been kicked and had his bowl taken away.

'I'm sorry mate.' I reached across and gave his wrist a reassuring squeeze. 'It's the jet lag hitting me already, I think. Made me a bit cranky.'

'It's fine Ruben. We're all a little scared.' He smiled at me.

Fuck he was right. I was more than a little scared.

CHAPTER 4.

Making my way to the luggage hall I had stumbled across a smoking room and decided to go in and take a couple of cigarettes in after thirteen odd hours without one. The bags took an age to come out in England so thought I'd have a while out here as well.

I should have taken the orange and brown windows as a sign of what was to come inside and the hint that this wasn't going to be a pleasant experience. Inside was like a cremation chamber. The small suction fan looked as if it had given up the ghost years before. You could hardly see the person next to you. I considered sitting on the plastic seats, but you could almost see the tar sliding down the back. I licked my finger and ran it across the glass screen. It left a clean mark and a sick feeling in my stomach. There was no room to stub out the cigarette in the already overflowing ashtray. I noticed an old Thai man throw his on the floor and tread it out then instantly light another. I followed suit, minus the second Marlboro and pushed through the smog to the door. The fresh air outside the box almost made me pass out. It was like altitude sickness or the bens. My lungs felt like they would try to escape through my arse if I dared to go back inside one of those. Charlie would say that the Chinese invented them to torture prisoners. I was laughing at the idea when I realised that I couldn't see anyone from my flight. I'd been one of the first out. How long had I been inside that smoky hell? As I made my way to Passport control, I wondered if the Thai man had been trying to leave for a while but couldn't find the door and had simply resigned himself to a life in there where he would eventually die one day, and no one would ever find his brownish stained body. He would just blend into the surroundings. I thought about telling Charlotte about the box if I bumped into her again before she left with Bernie.

The luggage hall was packed with hundreds of backpacks all moving in the same directions. It was actually rare to see a proper suitcase. I made a point to go out of my way and try to find one. I smiled at the first person I saw. They looked at me like I had some sort of mental disorder. I checked which belt my bag was coming on and looked for the nearest toilet.

After the smoking box I wasn't holding out too much hope for the cleanliness of the toilets but was pleasantly surprised by what I found. The urinals were cleaner than most you would find in public toilets in England. I popped my head into a cubical and the pans were almost sparkling with new rolls of paper. Now, fuck knows how they would look in an hours' time or whether the cleaner had just walked out but at that moment they were clean and that's all that mattered. I'd have happily taken a time out there. I washed my hands, soap smelled like something you could only buy in Marks and Spencer.

I still couldn't see Charlotte as I made my way through customs. I had nothing to declare other than this was the moment I was looking forward to the least. Even after over thirteen hours packed into a metal tube with hundreds of people I'd never met before, breathing their recycled air, eating shit food, and drinking miniature bottles of whiskey like a hobbo. This moment terrified me the most. Having to walk out into the melee of the arrival's hall.

I hoped she hadn't left me for dead and decided Bernie of all people would be a better travelling companion than me. I became so transfixed on the notion that she could leave me here alone that I hadn't realised I was already stood in the middle of what seemed like a thousand Thai taxi drivers all trying to catch my attention. Not only mine but it felt that way. I turned in circles looking for the way out, desperately trying not to make eye contact with any of them. It was oppressive and terrifying but also slightly exhilarating at the same time.

I felt a gently squeeze of my elbow. It was soft so I didn't try to tear my arm away.

'Come on, let's get a taxi together. I'll drop you on the way.'

I looked at Charlottes face. She was the calm in the storm. Amongst the madness and shouting in broken English she seemed serene. I wanted to kiss her and hold her. I wanted to run outside and cry, but she soothed those feelings away with that beautiful smile and the kindest of touches.

'Where's Bernie?' I shouted. I didn't really care but knew I should ask.

'He's gone in with someone else. He got talking to them at the belt.'

'Who?'

'Don't know. A couple of fellows from Manchester.' She ushered me through a gap in the crowd. 'Is that really your bag?'

I swung my Berghaus around and smoothed the side down. 'Yeah. Why?'

'No reason. I suppose it would have been strange if you had a normal backpack like everyone else.'

I didn't get what she meant so left it there. Leaving the airport building we ended up in the middle of even more men shouting at us. I stood frozen, not knowing what to do. In London I'd have been fine, but it was different here. Hardly anyone spoke English.

'The taxi rank is this way.' She nodded her head to the right. I followed.

The ride into Bangkok was nice. Relaxing even. After being squashed into a seat meant for children for half a day the inside of this air-conditioned car felt like paradise. The leather seats were an added touch of luxury. The scenery to be fair was shit. Lots of warehouses and apartment blocks that looked unfinished. I'm still not sure what I was expecting on the way into a major capital city. Maybe some idyllic paddy fields or jungle. It was the drive from Heathrow through Hammersmith. Just a lot hotter. I looked across the back seat to Charlotte she was gazing at the grey buildings shooting past us. Her window was all the way down despite the air-con blasting into us. I thought maybe she was too cold and was trying to let in some of the warm air. The wind was blowing her hair so that she kept having to push it back and keep her hand on top of her head. I loved her hair, long to her shoulders and dark brown with a slight hint of a wave through it.

'Where you from?'

I looked at the driver's eyes in the rear view mirror.

'Um, London. England.' I almost instinctively replied "And you?" but realised that would be stupid.

'You know David Beckham?'

'I'm sorry?' I was annoyed at him for breaking my daydream of Charlotte.

'Mr Beckham. You know?'

'No. Why would I know David Beckham?'

'He from London like you.'

I laughed at the thought. 'No, sorry but I've never met him. London is very big.'

He seemed upset. 'Ok.'

I realised Charlotte had stopped watching the buildings and was listening to my strange conversation.

'This is amazing isn't it?'

'What is?'

'This.' She motioned around the taxi and the motorway outside.

'OK.' I said

'Don't be negative. It's brilliant, look.'

I glanced out of the window in case I had missed something while discussing me not knowing Beckham. I could have been in Crawley other than a few palm trees and signs in a foreign language. I shrugged my shoulders.

'Really?' She looked upset. 'You don't find any of this cool?'

I grimaced slightly at the use of the word "cool".

'Not really. I'm sorry but we're in a cab driving down the motorway surrounded by shitty looking buildings. I'm hoping things get better to be honest. I could have gone to Birmingham for this.'

'Such a wanker. How about being asked if you know Beckham just because you're from London?' The driver looked up at the mention of his hero's name.

'Thought it was a bit strange to be fair.'

She laughed and looked out of the window again not answering. She also reached across and pulled my hand to the middle seat so she could hold it comfortably. The driver was still staring at me.

'Seriously, I don't know him.' I said.

He let out a little sad sigh and went back to driving. I rested my head back and enjoyed holding Charlottes hand. It was incredibly soft. I turned her hand over her nails were manicured. I needed a cigarette and some sleep.

The rest of the journey to the city went by in pretty much silence. Other than the driver asking if this was our first time in Thailand no one spoke. Charlotte tried to absorb everything that flashed past and I tried not to ruin it for her. The driver let me smoke a cigarette out of the window for an extra one hundred Baht. I didn't know how much that was but happily agreed.

As we entered the city proper the traffic became more intense. The little tuk-tuk's buzzed us looking for their next fares or to drop off drunken tourists.

'Are you sure you don't want to stay in the hotel with me?' I said. I wasn't sure if it was more for my benefit than hers.

'No, Ruben. I reckon I'll be fine. Anyway, I don't know you from Adam. I'm not going to share a room with you.'

'What about the plane? The kiss?'

'It was just a kiss Ruben.'

'I suppose so.' I was blushing. 'I'll probably fall straight to sleep when I get into the room anyway.'

'You are hilarious Ruben.'

It started to annoy me that she kept using my name in almost every sentence she directed at me. It wasn't needed. 'Why's that?'

She didn't hear me. Her attention had been drawn to a small elephant walking along the pavement. I thought she was going to climb out of the window. Once I had noticed the elephant, I couldn't take my eyes of it either. The elephant would stop at tourists to have their photo taken and in turn they would throw some notes at the child in charge of the potentially dangerous beast. Where had I come to that an elephant, ok not a fully grown one, but a real fucking elephant can just be ridden down the middle of one of the capital cities streets. Or any of its cities or towns streets for that matter. I was hypnotised by it.

'Ruben can you believe there is an elephant right there on the street? I told you this country would be amazing didn't I.' She squeezed my hand. 'Can you believe it?'

'No, I can't. It's a bit sad though don't you think?'

She was frantically trying to get her disposable camera out of her bag. 'What do you mean?'

'Well, I doubt that animal enjoys being surrounded by fat

squalling tourists clambering all over it. I reckon the cars and motorbikes don't sound too pleasant either.'

'Such a kill joy.' The camera took a couple of quick shots then went back into her bag.

The lights turned green and we moved away from the crowd that had gathered around the poor fucker. A few hundred feet more and we made a left off the main Sukhumvit road.

'There are many roads in Bangkok called Sukhumvit. Each one had a number except the main Soi Sukhumvit. Strange isn't it?'

'Not really no.' I hadn't noticed her reading from her Bible.

'It stretches all the way from Bangkok to the border with Cambodia.'

'A bit like Watling street at home then?'

'Uh ha.'

She wasn't listening to me. She was engrossed in the pages. I watched the late afternoon sun bounce off of her Aviators. She bit her bottom lip to stop them moving when she read.

'We here.'

The taxi had stopped. I looked through the window to an impossibly white building. A porter came and opened the car door.

Charlotte laughed. 'I can see you will have some hardships here Ruben.'

'Are you sure you won't stay?'

'No, thank you but I'll be fine on The Road.'

'Ok, your loss.' I paused as I stepped out of the cab. 'How will I find you later? You didn't tell me where you were staying?'

'That's because I don't know the name of it yet. I know where you'll be so don't worry.'

She leant across the back seat and kissed me. I held the kiss as long as I could before she pulled back. I stepped out of the taxi.

The porter had put my bag on a trolly. It looked out of place on something designed to carry expensive suitcases. He closed the door of the car.

'Wait.' I said.

Charlotte leant out of the window. 'What's the matter?'

'Why?'

'Why what?'

'Why are all the roads named Sukhumvit?'

She laughed. 'I thought you had changed your mind about coming with me then. It's something to do with a civil servant who worked in transport.'

'Oh. Bit of a let-down. I thought it was going to be a King or Queen.'

'Nope not this time. See you soon Ruben.'

The taxi pulled away as soon as her head was back inside. Her armed waved a goodbye that I hoped wasn't forever. I should have gone with her. I felt like I was falling in love with her.

I turned to the porter who had been waiting a lot longer than he would have normally. He looked me up and down and realised the tip wasn't going to be large if at all.

CHAPTER 5.

Stepping into the cooled lobby area I looked around at the huge columns and the expansive reception desk. There were a few people in suits heading to the very nice-looking bar. Other than that, the only people here were me and the poor bastard pushing my bag on the oversized trolly.

'Sir, checking in is this way.' He gestured towards the desk. An impossibly beautiful women stood waiting for us.

'Thank you.' I said. 'You speak English very well.'

'Thank you, sir.'

'Where did you learn?'

I hadn't moved. I was transfixed by the height of the ceiling in there. It was easily four floors up. Maybe three.

'If you would like to follow me to the desk, sir.'

The porter walked away from me, obviously bored of waiting.

I find elevators an uncomfortable experience at the best of times. They have been around for decades and yet as a species we still have no proper etiquette for how to behave in them. Do you talk to each other? Should there be eye contact? Stand and face the walls? It's an anxious riddled way to travel. I prefer to take the stairs wherever possible. When I am forced into one, I always try a raise of the eyes and a smile as if to say "Well were here again, squashed into this tiny metal box being held up by some ropes. And at any moment we could plummet into the pit at the bottom and be smashed to pieces but let's not make it awkward." I'll then spend the entire time staring at my feet desperately trying not to cough. I sometimes cough when I am nervous or in uncomfortable situations.

My ride up to the tenth floor had no chance for idle chit chat. Or any moment for eye contact. The porter took my key card from me, you needed it to operate the lift, pressed level ten and faced the door. There was no more interaction. On level seven the doors opened to a young couple. Before they could step inside and join the misery my jolly companion raised his hand.

'We are going up. The next elevator will be along shortly to the right.'

They were as stunned as I was. 'Bad day.' I said to them as the doors closed.

I returned to listening to the dreadful piped in music. The tune was familiar, but I couldn't place it due to the re-recording in a classical way. I started humming along trying to work out what it was. The porter glared at me as if trying judge where to hit me first. I hummed quieter.

The doors finally opened. 'Tenth floor, sir.'

'Thank fuck for that.' I pushed past him still humming.

We walked to one end of the long corridor. '1009.' He swiped the card and pushed the door open.

It was a nice room. Huge double or King bed, not sure which. TV on the wall, I picked up the remote and made a show of studying it.

'The bathroom, sir.'

I turned back to the porter and walked into the room he had opened the door to. He was right, it was the bathroom, and it was very large. Just above the bath was a type of window shutter that you could open while you were having a dip and see the city outside. I slipped my trainers off and climbed in the tub. Resting my head back I stared through the strange internal window. It was a nice idea, just a bit weird. I realised he was looking at me lying in an empty dry bath and it dawned on me how ridiculous I appeared. I clambered out and went back into the main room. He talked me through the services that the hotel offered and the specials on the room service menu.

'Can I order something now?'

'Yes, sir. Just dial nine and it will put you through to the restaurant.'

'Great.' I said sitting on the edge of the bed. It felt like a cloud.

'If there is nothing else, I can help you with I will leave you in peace. I hope you enjoy your time in Thailand, sir.'

'Yes, thank you.' I didn't even think that he may have other guests to deal with. 'Sorry, I should have asked before. What is your name?'

'My name?' He seemed shocked by the question.

'Yes. My name is Ruben.' I took a fifty Baht note out and held it in my outstretched hand.

'It's Alan.'

'Fuck off.' I said without thinking.

'I'm sorry.'

'Your name is Alan?'

He took the tip. 'Yes.'

'Is it your real name or one they make you use here? Make you sound more western for the guests.'

He laughed a little. 'Sir, my father was an avid English football supporter and he named me after his favourite player.'

This was better than the elephant. 'Who?' Alan started to relax.

'Sir, I really must be going.'

'Who?'

'Alan Hansen. He played for Liverpool and Scotland.'

'Alan fucking Hansen. You're kidding. I don't think even Alan Hansen's kids would want to be named after him.'

'Thank you, sir but I really must be going now.'

He thanked me again for the tip, I didn't know how much it was worth, and left the room. I sat back down on the bed and picked up the remote. I flicked through the channels until I became bored and turned the TV off again. Not knowing what I was supposed to be doing I opened the window and lit a cigarette inhaling hard. The smoke filled my lungs and instantly relieved any anxiety I had remaining. Bangkok seemed massive. It was manic at best and looking down to the busy streets below made you feel like you would end up a poster on rail station wall. Or a sex worker trafficked to a different country. I found the ashtray on top of the minibar and decided to help myself to a couple of bottles whiskey and a can of Heineken. Pouring both bottles into a glass I took a long slow drink and closed my eyes slumping onto the bed. This was as luxurious as it was going to be for the foreseeable future, but I was at peace. For the first time in months, fuck it years. I couldn't think of any immediate worry's that bore any relevance to my wellbeing.

I stubbed the Marlboro out lit another and went back to the opened window. Watching the people going about their daily lives I realised that Bangkok was just like London. It was another big capital with millions of people just wanting to get on with things in their own way. I've always tried to stay out of other people's way and not impact on them too much. Life is a struggle at the best of times and the least amount of interference from outside the better.

I dialled nine and ordered a pepperoni pizza and half a dozen beers. Laying on the bed I blew smoke rings to the ceiling till the cigarette burned my fingers. The whiskey didn't last long, and the small Heineken was only a few mouthfuls. I had noticed a 7/11 opposite the hotels entrance so changed into a pair of shorts and t-shirt and headed for the lift. The music inside the elevator was the same as before. I still couldn't place and tried singing along this time. The elderly couple I was sharing the ride with seemed nervous.

Alan was on the front steps wating patiently for the next guest to arrive.

'Just popping to the shop.'

'Yes, sir.'

'You don't really care, do you?'

'Not really, sir. No.' I loved his honesty.

Inside the 7/11 was so fucking cold I had to stand outside again without barely making the first aisle. I pressed my face against the window trying to work out the quickest route. I didn't need cigarettes so that would cut down the time needed at the till. I lit one of my duty frees and sat on the steps. The tiles were still hot from the day's sun and it took a few adjustments to get my shorts in the right place, so my legs didn't get too hot. I sat and watched Alan and the other porters checking the driveway and potted plants. One went through with a broom clearing any rubbish or sweeping the build up of dust away from the steps. Another came behind with a hose and wet everything down and watered the plants. It would have made more sense to water down the drive and steps first, but I didn't want to get involved. They took great care with what they were doing and showed a certain amount of pride in their roles that I envied. I once had a project manager who gave me one piece of advice that I have always stuck to. The man pushing the broom or cleaning the toilets is just as important as the man sitting behind the desk making the big decisions so respect them equally. Without either of them everything goes to shit.

I stubbed the cigarette out on the bottom of my trainer and took the plunge. Two minutes later I was back in the warm evening air, a bottle of VAT 69 and a packet of condoms in hand. You never know I had said to the apathetic teenager behind the counter.

I went back to my room on the tenth floor and drank until my dinner arrived. The waiter wheeled the trolley into the centre of the room and with some showmanship lifted a large white napkin to reveal an actual pizza box underneath. The waiter was staring at me and grinning like he had a hard on. Don't get me wrong I was never expecting a proper pizza box from room service, but his reaction was a little too much and left me feeling slightly nauseous.

'Thank you.' He didn't make any movement for the door. 'I can manage from here I think.'

'Ok, you have lovely evening sir.'

He still didn't move. He just stood there, his eyes darting between me and the box.

'Do you want a slice? I'll be honest I probably won't eat it all anyway.' I opened the lid.

'No. Thank you. You very kind.'

The pizza smelt amazing. If I were him, I'd have taken a slice and happily fucked off. He looked very thin under his white suit and gloves. It was the first time I had noticed the white gloves. I opened one of the beers he had brought up and took a long slow drink keeping one eye on the waiter who was now bordering on the intruder category. He wouldn't leave. I routed through my pockets for some notes when it hit me.

'Strawberry Fields.'

'Sorry sir?'

'It's the fucking Beatles.' I hummed a section. 'In the lift. Strawberry Fields.'

I sat on the bed picking up a slice of pizza and sang a few lines. The waiter became nervous and left quickly. Thailand was turning out to be quite nice.

CHAPTER 6.

Four days in and I was struggling. Not with being in Bangkok or finding something to do. Bangkok was an amazing city. I had visited a few Wat's, Buddhist temple in laymen. Taken a boat trip down the Thai version of the Thames. It was the doing all that stuff on your own. Breakfast, dinner going to a market on your own gets a bit pathetic after a couple of days.

I had found a little place to have breakfast, it was two roads away from the hotel. The first morning I sat down the girl serving me came to the table and asked if my wife would be joining me.

'She's sleeping. Jet lag.' I still don't know why I had lied.

She didn't really care. 'You want order?'

'Yes, please. French toast and a Coke.'

'Your wife come later?'

'No, I doubt it.' I was a sad loser.

This went on every time I went in there. Even at dinner time the same questions.

'Where your wife? She not well?'

'No, the jet lag has made her ill.'

I knew they knew I was lying. And it was confirmed to me at breakfast by another patron. He leant across from the table to the left. He had been happily shovelling eggs down his throat and smoking a cigarette at the same time. I found this disgusting. A friend I had for a while in my late teens used to do the same thing. We would go to a local café on a Sunday morning after spending all night at a house party and boast about the amount, of drugs we had consumed or girls we had slept with. He would cut up the ingredients of his full English into small pieces and use a spoon to eat. With every mouthful he would take a drag from the cigarette. It would make me gag.

'I was listening to them talking about you yesterday.' He sounded like he was from Yorkshire somewhere. 'They don't believe the wife story.'

'Really. Do they speak English to each other then?'

'Ha.' Resting the near butt in the ashtray he held out his hand. 'I'm Dave, and no they don't speak English to each other when no one is around.' He paused looking very pleased with his self. 'I speak fluent Thai.' He made a weird laugh noise that seemed too high pitched to have come from any human.

What a cunt I thought. 'Good for you. What did they say?'

'I'm not really at liberty to reveal that but let's just say they have an idea you are here alone.'

I wanted to tell him to mind his own business but other than Alan he was the only person to have spoken to me in days. I was starting to suspect Alan only spoke to me because he had to. I craved some interaction that didn't involve me handing money over.

The waitress put my coke down and removed the cap. Dave said something in Thai and she smiled at him. Although the smile didn't seem sincere. It struck me that I was not the only one who thought he was an irritating arsehole.

'Ok.' I said. 'Probably best if you kept it to yourself then. Wouldn't want you to lose their trust.'

I lit a cigarette and sipped at my coke. It was freezing but nice. I closed my eyes and blew smoke towards the street. The restaurant was one of the open fronted types and lead onto a very busy thoroughfare. I stared across the road to the massage shop opposite. I wondered what type of services they provided and whether the women enjoyed working there.

'So, Dave have you been in Bangkok long?' I thought I would give this being open to conversing to anyone a go.

'Well how do you define time in a place like Thailand?' I instantly regretted being so open. 'I mean look around you. These people have an air of mysticism about them. Everything is so calm, so tranquil that time seems have no meaning or relevance anymore.'

I wanted to pay up and leave but I was hungry and trying to find somewhere else that served decent French Toast could take hours. 'So, you've been here a while then?'

He tutted. I tutted back.

'Sorry…' A strange noise came from his throat. He was asking me my name without actually asking me the question. I was unsure whether to give my real name.

He was sweating even though the cool morning air hadn't given way to the obscene heat of the midday yet. I gave him a proper glance over for the first time. He was wearing some huge baggy trousers and a really shit t-shirt. He also didn't have anything on his feet. The beads braided into his matted hair was the nail.

Fuck it. 'Sorry Dave. It's Alan.' I didn't offer a handshake.

'Alan, Alan, Alan. A word of advice.'

The waitress put the French Toast down in front of me. 'Thank you.'

'Welcome.' She replied. A better response than Dave got.

'Let go. Just be yourself and see where the ride takes you. What works in the west won't work here.'

I poured some sauce on the side of the plate and cut a square off. 'Isn't that a line from a film.'

'No.'

'I'm sure it is.' The toast was good and worth listening to his drivel. 'It will come to me in a minute.'

'I don't think it is Alan. You must let yourself immerse into the spirit of what it is to travel these lands.'

'So, how long have you been in Bangkok? I've been here four days.'

He gave up. Far too easily to be honest. 'Bangkok for a month. Thailand for five.'

I took another sip of coke and checked my watch. It was eleven.

'I thought you could only stay for a month?'

'It's called a border run. Everyone who can't face going back does it.'

'Back? Back where?'

'Manchester. London. Stockholm. The fucking arse end of Wales. Anywhere you have to live like the rest of the heard.'

'Huh.' I turned to the lady behind the counter. 'Can I have two Chang beers please.' I thought it weird he had thrown in Stockholm but decided to leave it there. He was obviously passionate about the subject.

Finishing the coke and toast in silence I lit a cigarette. The waitress put the two bottles of beer down and removed the caps. It was still strange to me that they waited to take the lids off the bottles until they were on the table. She picked up my plate and walked away. I passed a bottle to Dave. He protested at first about it being too early in the day. That protest died when I told him the beer was on me.

'So, tell me more about the border runs and not living like the rest of the heard.'

CHAPTER 7.

I had left the increasingly annoying Dave sitting on a kerb trying to eat a chocolate crepe. He had been sick into his own lap
and that was my cue to go home. I had decided to go back and
have a night cap in the hotel bar. Wrongly, some might say I had
stolen Dave's weed from his bag while he was being sick. I'm
not proud of the move but it served a purpose. I smoked a joint
walking back making sure I stuck to the back streets so as not to
bump into any Police officers. I had heard the prisons out in this
part of the world weren't very accommodating to drug takers.

It hit me as I stepped inside the reception. Between the warm
Bangkok evening, the air-conditioned foyer and the strong
weed my head couldn't work out what my legs were supposed
to be doing. I stood staring into thin air for what felt like
an hour. Was probably around five or six minutes. They just
wouldn't move. It was like I had had a frontal lobotomy. There
is a scene from One Flew Over the Cuckoo's Nest, just after Jack
Nicholas has had one. If someone had taken my photo right,
then and there I would have been pulling the same face. I willed
them to take me forward.

'Is everything Ok Mr Humphrey?'

The ever present Hansen was clutching my left elbow. I had
started calling him Hansen in the hope he thought it endearing
and that he'd come for a drink with me.

'Which way to the bar?'

'Sir, maybe the elevator would be better.'

'Hansen help me to the bar please. I just need to sit down.'

'As you wish, of course.'

With his momentum to clear the reception before any of the more respectable cliental noticed me and I was in a seat bourbon in hand in no time.

'Please Mr Humphrey, ask the waiter to call me when you are ready to leave.'

I had no idea why this poor man suffered me. I would sit on the steps of the hotel and keep him company late at night though when the only guests coming in were the degenerates making their way back home after a night whoring in Nana Plaza or somewhere similar. Sex tourists aren't the most pleasant of people. I'd call them disgusting cunts given half the chance. I'm not the most innocent of people and I have had the privilege to have had sex with prostitutes, but these fucking people are literally here to only visit the red-light districts. He never really spoke to me while I was sat there smoking and drinking like a homeless person, but I know deep down he appreciated the company. This again was mainly for my benefit. The room although very nice felt oppressive at night. The walls closed in and I couldn't breathe.

The weed had begun to wear off after a while but now I was just drunk and alone. Sat in the cavernous, dimly lit bar I tried not to think too much. I wished I had brought a book with me or even a little music to distract me. It had been too long since I had last listened to some descent music. I called to the barman to play some Bob Dylan. He ignored me. Or didn't hear me. Or maybe I was still stoned and had imagined calling out but was actually mute. My head hurt. There were other people in here so decided to watch them as a distraction from the loneliness setting in. It was hard to make out features in this light.

I pushed myself up and made a stumble for the bar glass in hand. I waved to the young smartly dressed man behind. He walked very slowly towards me with a bottle of Jack Daniels. He had total contempt for me, and I didn't blame him. I stroked the rolled edge of the wood. It was beautifully made. Crouching slightly, I ran my eye the length of what I could see. It was perfect in every way. There wasn't a defect showing not a knot out of place. I was definitely still stoned.

'Just leave the bottle.'

'Sorry sir, but we don't do that here.'

I grabbed the bottle and winked at him. 'Don't worry. I know the management.'

'Sure, you do.' He said. He released his grip and walked away. Obviously paid too little to care about another pissed up, privileged westerner.

I filled my glass to the brim and faced the tables pushing the roundness of the bar edge into the small of my back. It felt like a massage. There was a young Indian looking couple sat in the corner. I hadn't noticed them before. They had a suspicious look to them that I didn't like. She was rubbing his leg and he kept eyeing the door. It was either that one of their respective others could burst through at any moment or their parents didn't know what they were up to.

I watched them for a few minutes, studying their moves. Every time her hand went too close to his probably by now very erect penis, he would push it away. She would then laugh and whisper something into his ear. It was very erotic. I took a large gulp of my bourbon. She made a play for his penis again. He appeared shocked and glanced around the bar like a wary gazelle at the watering hole. He noticed me looking and said something to the girl. She looked straight into my eyes and smiled. It turned me on, and I instantly wanted to be the one pretending that I didn't want her to touch me.

I drained what was left in the glass and refilled it setting the bottle carefully down on the bar. Rummaging around in my pockets I pulled a cigarette out and headed to the main entrance.

Alan was just finishing up the watering of the plants. I sat on the steps next to him and lit up. 'How are you feeling?' He said.

'Drunk. Although not the worst I've felt.'

'Good.'

He went about his chores and I watched him happily smoking.

'So, what are your plans?'

'What do you mean?'

'Surly you are not going to just sit in Bangkok until it is time to go home?'

'Of course not.' I had no plans. I was honestly thinking of doing just that. 'What would you recommend?'

He finished sweeping the steps and stood still resting on the broom handle. He looked tired. It was hard to tell his age due to the ill-fitting suit they made him wear but I put his age at around the early twenties mark. I finished the whiskey and searched for the bottle.

'Hold that thought Hansen, I'll be back in a minute.' Alan didn't appear to register what I had said but this had been the most we had spoken to each other and I didn't want it to finish.

Crossing the threshold of the bar I noticed the Indian girl sitting alone. She was playing with her fingers. Watching the way, she delicately twirled her rings between her slender fingers I was lost for a moment until I met her eyes. How long had I been staring? I moved to the counter where the bottle nestled. As I picked it up and turned her gentleman friend sat down opposite her with his back to me. I met her gaze again and smiled. She smiled back. I wanted to fuck her. I think she wanted to fuck me too. It could have been the drugs talking. I couldn't work out who was talking anymore.

'Would you recommend Kanchanaburi?' I asked.

'You could go there. Lots of foreigners do.'

I poured myself a glass and offered some to Alan. He didn't respond.

'Where is it though?'

'Slightly north west of Bangkok. You want to see the bridge?'

'Not really.'

'Why not? Your soldiers died building the bridge and the railway.'

'I know, but it's not the reason I'm interested.'

He didn't seem to care for my reasoning. He carried on sweeping and I slowly drained another glass.

'How would I get there?'

'Buy a ticket like everybody else.'

I couldn't work out if he were being sarcastic or rude, but he left me sitting on the steps and went back inside. I followed him a few minutes later. Inside the bar the Indian couple had gone, and the place was nearly empty. I called the barman over to settle the bill.

'How do I get to Kanchanaburi?'

This man hated me. I could see it. He wanted to smash the bottle over my head and take me out to the jungle somewhere.

'You go to train station or travel agent and buy ticket.'

I paid the bill.

'Where would I find one of those then?'

'What?'

'A travel agent. Or the station.'

He laughed. 'Buy a map.' He scooped up the money and turned away taking the bottle with him. I went to bed.

CHAPTER 8.

Bangkok's main station wasn't as bad as I first thought it would be. Pretty clean and well signed. My ticket and hotel had been sorted by a very nice girl in the travel agency right across the road from the hotel next to the 7/11. I didn't know it was there until Alan had shown me. I would like to say my farewell with Alan was an emotional one, but he simply carried my bag to the kerb called a tuk-tuk and walked away. It was a bit short considering he was my only friend in Thailand.

I found a bench on the platform my train was waiting on. There were quite a few other people with backpacks milling around. It gave me a sense of ease knowing I wasn't going to be the only westerner heading this way.

There is a lot of talk between backpackers of beating the unbeaten path. Being the first to go to a remote island or un-discovered village in the foothills of a mountain whose name cannot be pronounced. For some this is their whole life. They wear a badge of honour if they are able to tell you that they have already been to where you are heading. And they get a gold star if when they arrive, they are the first to discover this Shangri-la. I personally like the fact that I'm not going to be first there and that they will have properly flushing toilets in place and a bar that has the possibility of a decent glass of whiskey. That's not to say I would have trouble going alone.

The heat was already picking up. I checked my watch. It was only just past ten in the AM. I was looking forward to getting away from the heat and humidity of the city.

A train guard approached me and asked to see my ticket. I showed him and he pointed to a carriage off to the right. The carriage had seen better days. In fact, the train as a whole could have done with a lick of paint. You could see flecks of bluish grey below the green cover paint. The gold lines that should have run the full length of the carriages were hit and miss and the window frames appeared to be rotting away in places. The guard picked up my bag without warning and marched toward the direction he had pointed.

'Where are you going?' I shouted.

He kept walking. I jumped after him and grabbed the handle of my bag. He turned to me shocked at my intrusion.

'It Ok sir. I show you to your seat.'

'I'm fine thank you. I'll find it when I am ready.'

'No, no. I take you now.'

He snatched the bag back and double tapped away from me. I quickly went back to the bench and picked up my coffee and croissant and chased after the fleeing guard.

I managed to catch up with him as he opened the internal carriage door. The train was full. I couldn't see to the other end but there didn't appear to be anywhere to sit. I followed him anyway. Suddenly he stopped, looked at my ticket and started pointing and shouting at an old Thai couple. I couldn't quite work out what was happening for a few moments. There was a lot of gesticulating and shouting going around. After a couple of minutes, I noticed the hundreds of eyes that were firmly fixed on me and it struck. The old man, still protesting, pushed himself to his feet and held his hand out to his wife to help her up.

'No, please sit down. I'll sit somewhere else.'

'This is your seat.' The guard said to me. He barked at the elderly couple again.

'I really don't care. I'll find somewhere else to sit. Please let them sit back down.'

I tried to find support from my fellow passengers. There was none to be found. They either looked at me with pure hatred or a total disregard for the whole situation. I think most were just happy that it wasn't them being moved from the privileged white devil's seat. I made a clumsy attempt to ease the old man back into the seat, but the guard was not to be fucked with.

'No. This not his seat.'

He ushered them up again very unceremoniously. The couple shuffled off to the other end of the same carriage and sat down. The guard thrust the ticket back into my hand and dropped the bag.

'I could have taken their seat.' I protested.

He walked away leaving me with the eyes that were now piercing my skull. I sat down on the worn out wooden pew and sipped the scalding coffee burning my lip. It was disgusting but gave me something other than the situation to focus on. The seat made my arse hurt already.

CHAPTER 9.

As the train laboriously pulled from the station, I craved a cigarette. The journey would only take around four hours they told me. The sound coming from the engines as we struggled through Bangkok suggested otherwise. Finishing the last of my coffee and croissant I thought of Charlotte and whether she would pick up the letter I had left for her at the reception desk. I took a cigarette out and twirled it through my fingers.

'No smoking. You go to door.'

A young man opposite was pointing towards the rear door of the carriage. I looked behind me in the direction in question and caught the eyes of the old couple I had evicted.

'Can you watch my bag please?' I nodded upwards to the rack above our heads.

'Sure.' He replied with a certain indifference.

I knew he would rifle through my belongings as soon as I left. Probably to the delight of his fellow countryman. I grabbed my smaller bag that carried everything of value and headed to the back avoiding those loaded stares. Once I closed the door I glanced back to my seat. My bag wasn't in the rack. The bastard had barely waited for me to leave the carriage.

The guard tossed a butt through the open door as I approached.

'Excuse me.' I said offering another. He smiled and took one gratefully. 'It's ok if I sit here?'

He shrugged and walked away so I sat myself down on the steps and lit up inhaling deeply. I pulled a small bottle of local whiskey from the bag and took a long hit. It wasn't too bad. I couldn't pronounce the name. It soothed my head.

Watching the first villages outside the city glide past was relaxing. Children tried to run alongside and waved to me. Despite the fumes and dust, it was a calming experience being sat there on the metal stairs watching the Thai countryside fly past. As we approached the villages the train would slow down. This gave me a chance to see between the huts and buildings properly. Children playing, children crying. Mothers going about their daily chores and chatting and laughing with their neighbours. I imagined them discussing what was happening in the world, how their husbands were spending too much time in the pub. They were like every other village, town, hamlet, or street in the world. Places to be, jobs that needed doing.

I lit another Marlboro and pulled a copy of the letter I had left for Charlotte from my pocket. I'm still unsure why I made a copy of the letter let alone wrote one in the first place. I thought it would be romantic I suppose. I took another long swig of the whiskey and read the letter.

Dear Charlotte,

I'm sorry I didn't come and find you. I did visit Koh San Road but there were so many people that I freaked out and left. What's the point of coming all this way to just sit in a bar watching pirate copies of shit films you wouldn't watch at home? It doesn't make sense. It looked like a fucked up version of the UN. I think almost every country in the world had a representative there. Maybe they should transfer the decision making to that road instead.

I thought I would write you a letter rather than leaving a message with reception. People don't write letters anymore. Have you noticed? Why sit down and write a letter when you can send an email or cram your message into fifty characters on a text? I find it easier to explain things on paper than I do in person.

I like you Charlotte. You make me feel at ease, which is a rare thing for me. I can't stop thinking of that kiss on the plane. I've only spent a few hours with you, but I hope to spend a lot more time with you while we're out here.

Have you thought of visiting Kanchanaburi? I'm heading there as I have something I need to do. Obviously, I'll visit the bridge too. Did you know that supposedly it's not the original bridge? Not sure if that's true. I've booked into the Hotel Lotus if you're interested. It has a Wild West themed restaurant and a nightclub. I'll be there a few days before heading up to the Laos border. I've heard Luang Prabang is beautiful and sits on the Mekong river. It should be cooler than Bangkok.

Did you like Bangkok? I thought it was manic but enjoyed what I saw of the city. The boat ride down the Chao Phraya was amazing. I even went to the floating market, that was a bit shit. There was another one where you could buy live animals in little cages. I'm sure I saw monkeys there. I didn't like that.

Met a really nice Thai man called Alan. He was named after Alan Hansen. Madness. I'll introduce you if I get the chance.

Anyway, I have a train to catch so I'll end it here. I hope to see you soon. I wonder if Bernie has evaporated yet.

Yours sincerely

Ruben.

It was a good letter I thought. I had considered ending it with an "all my love" but changed my mind. I was glad I hadn't. I folded the paper and tucked it back inside my jeans. Leaning back against the open doors I settled in for the long haul and contently watched as Thailand sped past me in a blur.

CHAPTER 10.

What can I say about Kanchanaburi from my first impression. Only that it was a bit of a shithole. The station wasn't very big and had dogs roaming around probably looking for abandoned children to drag off into the undergrowth. And the streets around the station looked grubby to put it mildly.

The taxi driver dropped me half a mile from my hotel. No reason given I think he just couldn't be bothered to complete the journey. It was nice to stretch my legs though after the long-time spent on the train. I had lost a few t-shirts from my bag to the very friendly compatriots I had shared the carriage with. In fact, the old man who's seat I had taken actually wore one of my t-shirts over his shirt.

'Just walk. Not far.' The taxi driver had shouted while waving his hand in the direction of the hotel.

So that's what I did. I walked. I stood waiting at a set of traffic lights. Motorbikes and Tuk-Tuk's flew by without a care in the world. I kicked a piece of metal that caught the sunlight. Turned out to be a used bullet casing. Not waiting for the lights to fully change I picked up the pace to the hotel.

The western style restaurant was large, open air and not very Wild West. The only real nods to the American West era were the cowboys on the menu, the oversized wooden carriage wheel that hung above the bar and being called "Wild Bill's". The staff weren't even dressed in the correct clothes.

I sat back in my chair and lazily smoked a cigarette sipping my large glass of Chang Beer. There was a great breeze coming through keeping everything cooled. It had been a hot day and the sun going down didn't bring the respite it should have. By the time I had reached the hotel earlier that day the sweat had been uncontrollable. The porter who had shown me to my room had turned the air-conditioning on and left me laying on the bed almost hyperventilating. He was no Alan.

Stubbing the cigarette out I thought about Alan and wondered what he was doing right now. Hopefully, he was staying out of trouble. I wondered further if he had met Charlotte yet. If she had come to the hotel to pick up the letter. I could see them both sitting outside where I would sit, Charlotte reading my very impressive letter and her and Alan sharing an anecdote or two about me. Alan wouldn't say much as he was a man of little words. When he did speak though he was wise beyond his years.

'You ordered?'

I glared at the waitress, looked her up and down. From her cheap black pumps to her ill-conceived red lipstick. How dare you interrupt my daydreaming. 'I'll take the Calamity Jane burger please.'

'You want extra cheese?'

I thought for moment and sipped my beer. This could be the difference between a good night's sleep and waking at four in the morning with heart burn.

'Please.' She walked away her job done. She was cute. I like the way her arse moved. I felt bad for the way I had dismissed her so quickly.

On the other side of the restaurant was a large group. They all seemed centred around an elderly white man in a wheelchair. The only non-white face there was a young man sat on the right hand side of the wheelchair. He was smartly dressed in a two piece suit with his hair perfectly parted on the side and gelled into position. I lit another Marlboro and studied the group. They were a mix of men and women of varying ages. It looked like it was the old man's birthday. He couldn't have been younger than eighty five if a day. He had an oxygen tank next to him and a huge cigar in his mouth. Ironic I thought and stupid.

The waitress caught my eye and smiled. I smiled back and tapped the side of my bottle. Not in a master, servant way but just to say I needed another without her needing to walk all the way over to me to find that out. She was actually very attractive. She had beautiful eyes and dead straight black hair to her shoulders.

My focus went back to the group. There was something off with the young fellow. Why was he there? The rest of them seemed normal enough. Expensive looking clothes, Ray Ban glasses. Studio levels make up. Where he appeared to be an intruder invading another's celebrations and they were too well mannered, too high brow to tell him to fuck off. His clothes and hair made him fit, but something just wasn't right.

The waitress came over with my food and drink. It was an enormous burger. I asked her to bring me an extra bottle of beer. She said sure in a weird American accent and walked away. I noticed that she had a Led Zeppelin t-shirt on under her overly starched uniform white shirt. I smiled thinking how much I'd like to see her in just the t-shirt.

After a few mouthfuls I was done with the burger. It was good but too greasy. I wished I hadn't had the extra cheese. I went back to watching the side show. It was hypnotic. Here was this rogue agent in amongst these people and I seemed to be the only one who could see him. There was a little panic in the back of my mind that he was in fact a ghost and I was slowly going mad. One of the women to the left of him made a passing glance in his direction which eased my tension a little. Her eyes were full of hate for him. It was as though she had just seen the person who had broken into her house, killed her kids and fucked her dog while she was at work.

The waitress came back and broke the spell. It was annoying.

'Something wrong with the food?'

'No. I'm tired and not as hungry as I thought.'

'Here's your drink.'

I had forgotten about the drink. She picked up my plate. 'Thank you. Can I ask you a question?'

She followed my eyes. 'You don't want to know.'

She turned and walked away but this time I didn't watch her very perfect arse dance across the restaurant. I did want to know. I wanted to know everything that was happening in this sordid TV show that was being played out in front of me in real life. Who was the stranger in the camp and why did the woman want to bathe in his blood.

'Fuck it.' I hadn't meant to say it out loud.

I pushed myself off the chair lit a cigarette and headed straight for them. At the last second, I diverted off and stood just to the left of their table. Trying to be as nonchalant as I could I stole quick glances and tried to listen to their conversation. The whole time I pretended to be inspecting the traffic tearing past. There was nothing untoward that I could make out, so I stubbed my cigarette out on the ashtray on the table next to them.

I caught the eye of the boy as I made the move back past them. He couldn't have been older than sixteen, seventeen max. I smiled at him and he tried to return the same but failed halfway and instead showed pain in his face. Something drew my line of sight down. The old man's hand was stroking the boy's thigh. I stared at this action for far too long than I should have. The TV programme had suddenly turned into an expose of the crimes against children. It was a car crash that my head wouldn't turn away from.

'Can we help you?' It was one of the women. Around fifty. She was glamorous but you could tell she didn't need to try. More Jane Fonda then Liza Minnelli. She sounded Spanish but could have been Portuguese. The hand had stopped moving and I realised the whole table was now staring in my direction. Twenty eyes waiting for an explanation as to why I had interrupted their night out.

I looked straight at the boy ignoring her question. 'Are you ok?'

He nodded and smiled. This time with a little less pain. 'Yes. Thank you.'

'What are you implying?' This time one of the men were on his feet. He seemed pissed.

'Nothing. You people have a lovely evening and enjoy your meal.'

He stayed on his feet until I had sat back down and then slowly descended back into his own chair. The whole time watching to see if I made a move.

I ordered another beer and a whiskey for the side. It sickened me to think that the boy didn't want to be there. The waitress came over with the drinks.

'That was kind of you.' She said.

'What was?'

'Actually, showing you cared he was ok. Most farang's don't.'

'Farang's?'

'Sorry. Foreigners. Westerners. Most come, take what they want and don't think of the mess they leave behind or who they hurt. If some thought of the lives they destroy it might make a better country for us.'

I raised my glass to her and downed it in one. 'There are still some good ones out there. Sometimes I feel like I'm holding the fort all on my own though.'

She laughed and walked away. I took out the letter I had written for Charlotte and re-read it. The words seemed stupid and incoherent now I was drunk. It would normally be the reverse and the idea of leaving a letter would seem romantic and be the start of a new love story for the ages. If Charlotte had left a letter like this for me, I'd have run a mile. Lighting the corner of the page I tossed the paper into the ashtray as if doing this would make the original a few hundred miles away suddenly vanish. I watched the words burn. The waitress brought a large whiskey over and gently slid the glass in front of me careful to avoid the tiny bonfire I was having.

'Thanks, but I didn't order that.'

'It's from your little friend over there.'

I looked over to the table. He smiled and raised his glass. The pain had ebbed slightly from his face and he seemed a bit happier. I nodded my appreciation and he turned back to the conversation that was happening around him but that he had no involvement in. I watched and wondered how much of what was being said he could understand.

'For you.' The waitress slipped a piece of paper under my glass and went back to clearing tables.

Her name was Achara. I pronounced it how it was spelt. Probably wrongly. There was a little message that I worked out was asking for my room number. She had left a pen. I loved her promiscuous approach. I smiled and considered the offer. I was very lonely and could do with the company. She was also extremely beautiful. I looked at the burning paper in the ashtray and twirled the plastic pen between my fingers waying up the possible outcomes.

I asked for the bill still unsure. She brought it over in a small leather folder, turned and walked away. I took my wallet out and pulled the Baht from the back. A piece of paper fell on the floor. Reaching down I realised it was Charlies' last number. I had forgotten that I had it. Studying the numbers for an age I considered adding it to the dying bonfire. Instead, I neatly folded the paper and put it back from where it had come. Leaving the money, I stood and walked towards the front doors of the hotel. As I reached the entrance, I looked back to see Achara pick up the secret note and hold it close to her face to read.

Room twenty-one, second floor. I headed upstairs for a shower.

CHAPTER 11.

'Do you change travellers' cheques?'

The man behind the reception desk was very smart and proper. His paperwork was in nice, neat piles and the staff around him looked terrified every time he spoke. I didn't know what it was with hotel managers.

'Excuse me…'

'My apologies sir. How can I assist you?'

I held my traveller's cheque high in the air. 'Do you change these?'

He barley took a side glance. 'No sir. I'm sorry. Not today.'

I looked towards the exchange rate board behind his head. He followed my gaze.

'Sir today is a holiday. All banks are closed.'

'But you're not a bank and I have no money.'

'Sir it is a holiday and banks are closed and we are not allowed to carry out any banking facilities.' He finally looked at me. 'That is unless you are changing Swiss Francs?'

'Why Swiss Francs?' Seemed an odd currency to pick. I'd have thought US Dollars.

'I take that as a no then. You can leave a credit card if you desire and run a bill with the restaurant.'

I fucking hated hotel managers. They were so smug and snobbish. Even the ones that ran shitty motorway service stop hotels that were basically legalised brothels had a certain air of being firmly up their own arse.

'Fuck it. I'll try somewhere else.'

'As you wish sir.'

I pushed the hotel's lobby door open and stepped outside. You could instantly feel the morning heat. It was only ten and already you could tell it was going to be a hot day. So much for getting away from the city heat.

Sitting on the steps I watched Achara going about her morning setting up duties. She moved with ease through the tightly packed tables and chairs. She almost danced between the gaps while carrying a huge basket of cutlery and menus carefully laying everything out and positioning the forks just so.

The previous few nights flashed through my memory. A blur of nakedness and Sangsom whiskey. Her body was amazing. She made me laugh and kept me intrigued with her stories about her home in the hills. We had sex on almost every square inch of that room. For three nights and days I couldn't get enough of her. When she worked, I would sit at one of the tables and watch her move. Toying with the customers making them believe that she was interested in them, that she wanted to know them more. I would constantly check my watch waiting for her shift to be over so that we could hide away in our room and dissolve further into one another. Love is a strong word that shouldn't be bounded around without due care and attention. Love in my eyes should be forever, whether you are in love or just have love for someone. Slightly idealistic I hear you cry. Infatuation is different. An infatuation can last from a fleeting moment to a few weeks or months. I knew this wouldn't last much more than a few days. I had to leave soon, and she had a life to get on with but for the brief time I had with her I wanted to take in as much from her as I could. I suppose I was being selfish in that way. Looking at my room afterwards it had a certain sadness. Empty whiskey bottles used condoms and broken dreams.

I lit a cigarette and slipped my sunglasses on. Achara finally noticed me and smiled. It made me feel wanted.

'Good morning.' I said.

'Sawadee.' She replied making a pray sign.

'I need to change this.' I waved the cheque. 'They won't do it in there.'

She turned her head to a waiting motorbike taxi driver and barked what sounded like an order. He dutifully nodded. She was amazing and somewhat of a bad ass. 'He will take you somewhere. Just be respectful to them.'

'Thank you.' I said and stole a quick kiss. She giggled and went back to laying tables for the next bunch of vagabonds to arrive.

I climbed onto the back of the waiting motorbike and he tore into the morning traffic before I had time to hold on. I had no idea where we were heading. The thought of my lifeless body raped and bloody lying in a ditch somewhere entered my head. After five minutes of weaving through the morning rush hour traffic I stepped off the bike and threw up into the kerb. My chauffer laughed showing his broken teeth. I retched again straightened myself up and faced the building I had been brought to. I couldn't see a bureau de change or any other type of money facilities. It was just a simple side street with non-descript building fronts. There weren't even any dogs.

I turned back to the taxi driver. 'What the fuck is going on?'

He stared at me. No emotion.

'If you even think of trying to rape me, I will kill you first.'

I was panicking. The thought of my used and abandoned body lying arse up by the side of this boring grey street wouldn't shift. I couldn't work out what troubled me more. The thought of being raped or the fact that my mind went straight to the thought of actually being raped by this man. I steadied myself, I was ready for the onslaught to begin. He didn't move other than to lean against his bike and light a cigarette. He looked me up and down like I was mad. Maybe I was.

'Come on then you bastard. You won't get my arse that easy.' There it was again. I raised my fists.

He smiled and pointed behind me. Turning slowly expecting the worst I was faced by a squat Thai lady chewing a toothpick. She was around mid-forties. Could have been older. Or younger depending on the light this light did her no justice. Behind her the door to one of the faceless shop fronts was open.

'Come in. No one going to rape you here. Unless you pay.' She screamed with laughter.

I took another look at the taxi driver. He still didn't move other than to flick his head towards the open door. Those awful broken teeth on show again. 'I wait.' He said.

Entering through the small door the room inside opened into a somewhere between a warehouse and a whorehouse. There were makeshift rooms scattered around the perimeter some with doors, others with just a curtain to hide the indiscretions that happened inside. A few of the doors were open and I could see massage tables and bottles of lotions. The strange bluish glow the lamps gave off mixed with the humming of the strip ceiling lights gave this place an air of mystery more in line with an underground bunker than whatever this place was. I could almost make out Hitler giving Eva Braun a pill just before the Red Army came bursting through the doors.

'You sit.' She pointed to a cheap looking leather couch pushed against one of the walls. 'And be good.'

I did as I was told. The couch squeaked as I sat down. I tried not to think of how many times it had been wiped clean. This place was becoming increasingly terrifying the more I looked.

'You want drink?'

'Yeah. Please.'

She stared at me. 'Well? I'm no mind reader.'

'Shit. Sorry. I'll take a whiskey if you have one.'

She screamed something into the empty expanse and not a few seconds later a very young girl appeared with my drink and placed into my hand.

'Thank you. How much?'

She didn't answer and walked away back behind one of the curtains. I took a sip of the drink and then noticed the table full of Thai men staring at me. I wasn't sure how I could have missed them in the first place but here they were confirming that I was in the wrong place.

'How you all doing?' Nothing but looks of disdain. 'What are you playing? Snap?'

One of them smirked and they went back to their game. Relieved at not getting shot I sipped more of the foul whiskey and slid the glass on the table in front of me. There was a huge glass ashtray in the middle so took that as an invitation to light up. Scanning the full inside of the building properly for the first time I noticed that it was actually a few buildings that had been knocked through into one huge space. Looking either side of me all the other door fronts had been bricked up years before so that the door I came through was the only way in or out to the street and safety. Everywhere else I looked were stacks of boxes containing anything from whiskey, beer and even children's toys.

The eerie atmosphere in this den of horrors was made worse by the feeling of more people here than I could see. I could feel them watching me. Faint footsteps echoed off the walls until they hit a column of boxes. I finished the whiskey and stubbed the cigarette out.

'Do any of you know where she went?'

The card sharps ignored me. One moved just enough for the glint of some sort of handgun to show beneath his jacket. Panic began to rise in my throat. One way out through a locked door and no one other than the toothless fucking idiot outside really knows I'm here. The young girl returned with a fresh glass and picked up the empty. I downed it in one my eyes fixated on the gun now very much on show. As she reached the table she slowly bent down and whispered something in the gun toting maniac's ear. He glanced across at me and calmly pulled his sports jacket closed.

'You scared of guns?' He said in such good English I almost asked "what gun." Instead, I smiled politely willing the woman to return quickly. She hadn't even looked at the cheque yet.

A couple more anxious minutes and the chain smoking of a few cigarettes I heard the shuffle of feet and the women appeared, huge grin and a plastic bag full to the brim with cash. As she passed the table, she patted the gunman on the arm to which he said something that made the whole crowd laugh and she released an ear-splitting noise. I knew that I was the joke. Mainly because she wagged her finger at me and called me a silly boy.

She sat down so close to me that she may as well have sat on my lap. She looked at my empty glass and screamed an order into the empty space again. It made me jump. The men didn't even react. This made her laugh.

'How much you change?'

'I have one hundred British Pounds.' I don't why I felt the need to say "British" Pounds. I couldn't think of any other types.

'Ah, rich man. No problem.'

The young girl brought over the newly ordered drink.

'Thank you.'

'You like her?'

'I'm sorry?'

'You like her? Take her, go boom boom.'

She made an horrific thrusting motion with her hips. It's an image I will never forget.

'Thanks, but I'll pass this time.'

'Ok. You like boys? I have boys.'

'Again, just the money this time.' I wanted out as soon as I could. 'Please.'

She snorted and flicked her head at the girl who scurried back into the darkness once more. 'You come to see the bridge?'

'Yes. Sort of. I'm heading that way as soon as we finish here.'

'You people.' She shook her head almost in disgust. Her cheeks wobbled. 'Only interested in the past. People who can't move forward don't move at all.' She rubbed her finger along the side of my face.

'Well, it's quite important to us.'

'It's past. Only important thing now is this.' She dropped the bag of money on the table. 'Show me cheque.'

I slid it across the table to her and she retrieved a calculator from somewhere in her arse.

'Ok. Exchange rate today is...' She gazed at the ceiling. I followed her eyes. There was nothing but dead insects and stains up there. 'I like you, so I give you sixty-seven Baht to your one British Pound.' She over emphasised the British part now.

'Well, it's not my Pound exactly. I think it belongs to the Queen.' I laughed at my joke. She didn't get it. 'Also, I think the banks are paying seventy.'

'Ok. You find a bank open today?' She laughed and slapped my thigh. It stung. 'We have deal or no?'

I would have liked to get up slap her back and walk out cheque in hand but that would have ended with a bullet in the back of the head and a shallow grave in the jungle somewhere.

'Deal.' I shook her hand as she let out the loudest laugh yet.

'You very handsome man. Maybe I give you a little go myself.'

'Just the money thank you.'

She stroked my hair. I dared not move. The man with the golden gun was watching us.

'Too much hair though.' She grabbed a handful and shook my head.

She set about counting the money into small piles. I had barley finished my drink and she was done.

'Ok. You have six thousand two hundred Baht.' She began putting the bundles of unused cash back in the bag.

'Sorry. You mean seven hundred? Should be six thousand seven hundred.'

She stopped moving the money and pushed my piles towards me. 'You think drinks are free? I gave you very good price for very good whiskey.'

'No but...'

She stopped me and cupped her hands around my face and pulled my head until we were almost touching noses. She was absurdly strong. Her breath smelt of whiskey and cigarettes. Although that could have been mine bouncing back.

'In this life darling nothing is free. Ok. There is always someone to pay.' She kissed me full on the mouth. I strangely enjoyed it. 'You pay me, I pay him.' She nodded towards the table. The man with the gun was still watching us.

'Who is he?'

She sniffed. A sniff is an underrated expression in my opinion. It can have just as many meanings as a laugh or a roll of the eyes. It all depends on the facial movements that accompany the sniff. Her sniff was one of hateful resignation.

'He fucking Police.' She sniffed again and spat on the floor. The young girl came running and almost caught the phlegm in mid-air. Mop in hand. I realised this poor young girl was some sort of forced worker. I think slave would have been too strong. She seemed well feed but there was definitely a lack of union access or even a Sunday off.

'Where is she from?'

She looked the girl up and down like she was looking at a dog. 'She Burmese.' She spat on the floor again.

The Policeman shouted something and both women stood to attention. They smiled a fake smile.

'You shore you don't stay?'

I looked at the table of men. They were probably all Police. 'No, I really need to go.'

'Ok handsome man. Sign cheque.'

I signed the cheque and made my way to the door.

'Hey. Enjoy the bridge.'

I pushed through the door to freedom. I didn't look back.

CHAPTER 12.

'Is this it?'

He didn't answer.

'John. Is this the bridge?' He nodded.

My motorbike taxi driver wasn't the most talkative fellow. After leaving the strange brothel warehouse I had asked him his name. He wouldn't or couldn't tell me hence the reason for me just calling him John. He didn't seem to mind. I would have loved to have been there when he told his family and friends about his new name.

I was slightly let down by the bridge. Not knowing what to expect I had a more show stopping vision in my mind. This just seemed a normal crossing. One you could find in any large town. There were dozens of tourists climbing all over it, so I joined in.

You have to step across the gaps between the sleepers which was unsettling at first. On either side of the track were small areas set back that you could shelter in should a train come. I stood and counted three on each side, each one only looked to be able to hold maybe six people at most and that's not counting a fat person with a backpack. I tried not to think what would happen if a train came and you couldn't make it to one of these safety zones or an obese lady blocked your way. Did you simply try to squeeze between the timbers and go for a swim?

I was thinking of whether I would fit through the gap when I noticed a young Asian couple trying to take a photo of themselves with the river as a backdrop. I tried to slide past them but a small boy on his hands and knees peering through to the river below trapped my escape. I considered shoving him to one side, there was no obvious parent around.

'Excuse me.'

Fuck. I knew they were talking to me without the need to look.

'Excuse me. Can you take our photo please.'

They were English which made avoiding this harder. I'd have to be rude or put on a really shit accent.

'Hello. Would you mind?' He was a persistent arsehole. He held out the camera.

'Sorry. I don't speak English.' I stepped over the boy making sure I trailed my foot and kicked him up the arse for causing me to be rude.

'Prick.' The young fellow shouted after me. 'Did you understand that?'

I kept walking to the other side of the river and turned in the direction I had come from. Not sure of what I was supposed to do now I lit a cigarette and sat down to the side of the tracks. Closing my eyes, I turned my face to the sun. It was hot here but without the stifling heat of Bangkok. I wished I had had some music. A little bit of Buffalo Springfield or a couple of Cream tracks would have gone down well.

'Hey prick, do you still not speak English?' I didn't open my eyes or answer. I just smiled and listen to all the other tourists doing the same thing.

Sitting next to the track made me think back to when I was around ten or eleven. Near to where I grew up was one of the main commuter lines into and out of London from outer Kent. It was surrounded by a few acres of woodland and would enter a tunnel just by a golf course. My friends and I would head in there during the school holidays. Someone had cut a hole in the fence and this was long before the tracks were lined with solid steel fencing.

We would sit around flicking through the porn magazines that always seemed to be lying around. One of my friends used to joke that nonces would stand behind the trees and masturbate while watching us reading the dirty magazines. It could have been true. The woods there had a horrible reputation of things happening to lone women and little boys who strayed too far. We would wait for the trains to come and six of us would line up with a handful of small stones and just as the train was about to enter the tunnel, we would let loose with everything we had at the windows. Hours was spent falling about laughing while re-enacting what we thought the commuter's reactions were.

When we tired of scaring the shit out of train passengers, we would go up onto the golf course and wait for the gentleman to tee off from down the hill. We would hide in the tree line and the closer you let the golfers get before you darted out and stole their ball decided how much bragging rights you had for the rest of the day. My favourite was to steal the ball without them seeing you. It was sometimes too much to bear watching them scratch their heads and hunt for something they could never find. My cousin used to run out and throw the balls back down the hill, also very enjoyable to watch.

After a while I ran out of cigarettes and was getting thirsty, so stood up and headed back across the bridge. As I stepped of onto the other side a very clean looking train pulled to a halt a few hundred yards from the bridge. I looked over to John and pointed to the train. He ignored me and went back to talking to some other taxi drivers. So fickle I thought.

I brushed my hand down the side of the carriages as I walked along the side. Dozens of very expensively dressed men and equally high classed women were disembarking and mixing with the normal tourists. Some were heading to the bridge while others were dabbing their heads with towels handed to them by porters and getting straight back on the train. None of them had paid this sort of money to mix with the commoners in this heat.

I tried to step onto the train and was met by the large hand of an even larger man. 'Can I help you, Sir?' He asked while holding his slab of meat on my chest. 'Are you a passenger?' He knew I wasn't. I was dressed like I had just gotten out of bed if that bed was under a hedge.

'No. But your colleague said it would be ok for me to come aboard and take a look around. Is that the right terminology "come aboard"?'

'Please leave.'

I stepped back from the train. This man looked like Thor. He was probably slightly bigger than Thor. 'Where are you from?' I asked.

'Australia.'

'Nice. Can I bum, a cigarette? I've run out.'

He leant in close. 'If you don't fuck off, I'll throw you from the bridge.'

Taking the hint and not wanting to see if he could throw me into the river I walked back along the track. One day when I was married to a Russian prostitute like the rest of the men on this beautiful train, I'd book a ticket back to the bridge.

'John, which way is the cemetery?'

All the taxi drivers stared at me. John thumbed over his shoulder.

'I'm going to buy some cigarettes and then we'll go.' He didn't have a clue what I was saying but I hoped he understood enough.

I bought two packs from the nearby kiosk and smoked one while I waited for John to finish his conversation. I made a point of stubbing the cigarette out, so he knew I was ready to go. Another few minutes, went by I lit another as it was evident by the beer John was now drinking that he was in no rush. I sat on his motorbike. He still didn't look over at me. I was like a child desperate for a father's attention.

'John.' I shouted.

He looked up and smiled sipping his beer. I put my hands on the keys and his face changed to an expression of anger and tiredness. It dawned on me that he was probably sick at having to trapes round after tourists all day and just wanted to enjoy a cold beer with his friends.

'I want to go to the cemetery.' Fuck what he wanted to do.

His friend passed him a cigarette. It was now a case of who would back down first. I hoped he would as I didn't want to try and steal his bike and I couldn't ride them anyway. He didn't move. Fuck it I thought and turned the keys. His face went to shear rage as he raced towards me and killed the engine snatching the keys away.

'No.' He shouted. 'Cemetery that way. You walk.'

I felt like a fool. Now I was the petulant child being scolded for not waiting and doing something stupid.

'Which way again?' I stepped off the bike.

He pointed off to the right. I handed him a hundred Baht and trudged off alone again and another potential friend lost.

After walking for about twenty minutes, I stopped at a café overlooking the river and had a couple of beers. It was past midday, and the temperature was well above thirty degrees. A gentle breeze came off the river and cooled the café naturally. I had just started reading a new book, so it was nice to sit in the relative quiet of the near empty café and escape myself for an hour or two.

The cemetery was morbidly beautiful. Surrounding the lines of headstones, the perfectly uniformed grass was so pristine and equal you could take a ruler to any blade and come up without a defect. This was a place of honour. Somewhere only heroes were laid always in touching distance of the ground they gave everything for.

I walked each line carefully reading every inscription. Men in their late teens and early twenties taken in the best years of their lives for areas of the world that they probably couldn't have spelt the names of let alone point out on a map. I eventually came to what I had been looking for. This stone was over near the back and four in from the left. I knelt down in front of it.

'So, you were Grandad's brother.'

Jack Humphrey, Private in the Royal Artillery. Just another name in this sea of soldiers. My Grandad spoke fondly of him. They had been true friends as children. When the war came, they had both signed up to the Royal Artillery together. Jack had been sent to the Far East to defend Singapore or somewhere and my Grandad had ended up in Italy. He was in Bari Harbour when the Nazi's bombed it. Thanks to our dear American friends there was also a ship full of chemical weapons that they had sailed into port and had forgotten to tell their allies about. My Grandad had ended up in hospital with some form of gas poisoning. He could virtually speak fluent Italian by the time he left so every cloud and all that. Poor Jack had been forced marched from Singapore up here to die in this sweaty hell hole so he could build a shitty railway that wouldn't help the Japanese win the fucking war anyway. Such a futile waste of so many young men for a few miles of metal tracks in the jungle.

I took a bottle of Jack Daniels from my bag raised it to the stone and took a long slow drink. I laid down next to the grave and lit a cigarette.

'Hope you don't mind if I smoke Uncle Jack.' I laughed. And then I cried.

I told Jack everything. About Charlie and how I still thought I loved her. About the drinking and the drug taking. I even told him about the dreams. Shit I hadn't really spoke about them to anyone, but I poured it all out and cried until I was exhausted and drunk. The bottle was empty. I swung myself onto my knees and rested my forehead on top of the stone. It was cool. 'Thanks Jack. For everything. My Grandad never forgot you.'

I kissed the stone. I don't know why I did it and felt a bit stupid afterwards. I even looked around to make sure no one else would have seen me do it. Standing I picked up the butts and put them in the empty bottle. I had to get back to Bangkok to catch a train up to Chiang Mai. I wanted to be in Luang Prabang in a few days. I also needed to write my letter to Charlotte. At the gates I caught a proper taxi back to the hotel. I was tired and burnt.

CHAPTER 13.

Dear Charlotte,

I hope you are well and keeping safe. Did you get my last letter? I suppose you wouldn't be reading this one if you hadn't. Did you get to meet Alan? He's hilarious. I hope you haven't checked into this hotel it's a bit shit. Find somewhere to else to stay.

I'm heading back to Bangkok before I catch the train north to Chiang Mai. I've booked a place called MD Hostel. Looks nice and has a pool. I'll only be there a couple of nights before heading to the border. If you haven't caught up to me by then I suppose we will bump into one another at some point down the line.

Kanchanaburi isn't that bad. Make sure you don't use one of the motorbike taxis to take you to change money. There's one that hangs around this hotel who's a real bastard.

I managed to see my great Uncles grave. It was slightly surreal. I had a drink with him and a good chat. Not as weird as it sounds. Maybe it is. It's strange that he is buried all the way out here. My Grandad had told me once that their Mum had always wanted to bring his body back home. That he should be close to his family, but my Grandad said he should lay next to the men he fought and died with. I personally don't see the difference where your body is buried. You can bury my heart wherever you want. I'll be dead so it won't much matter.

Anyway, hopefully you catch me in Chiang Mai. It's lonely on your own don't you think.

Yours Sincerely

Ruben.

CHAPTER 14.

I've honestly tried to think of something good to say about the train journey to Chiang Mai. I still can't. It was long, uncomfortable, and sweaty. Also, so boring I could have jumped from the roof at least a dozen times. This ride had really started to compound the whole travelling lie number two. The journey is not always the best bit. It's fucking tedious.

Finally stepping off fourteen hours after getting on in Bangkok was like being born again. I was hungry and tired and wanted to cry. Having only packed a tube of pringles and a bottle of water for the entire trip I could have eaten one of the stray dogs by the time I reached the hostel.

The room was basic but nice. Bed, toilet, shower, and ashtray. It even had a TV. The only English Channel was BBC World News, but I've always liked the news so win, win in my book. There is nothing worse than someone who has no idea of what is happening around them. Yes, most news is doctored slightly depending which way the newspaper or TV station leans but you can get a gist of the state of the World from it. I smoked two cigarettes, one joint and ate another tube of crisps. Sleep came easy that night. A mixture of shear exhaustion and being stoned worked wonders.

As soon as I woke, I dressed in my swimming shorts and headed to the pool. I had briefly seen it on my way in the night before, but it had been dark, so I didn't pay too much attention. I couldn't wait to sink to the bottom. There were a few others around the pool. I don't like getting to a pool when other people are already there. It makes me feel like I'm imposing on them.

I also have the feeling that they are watching me and sizing me up. A couple around mid-thirties sat in the far corner. They kept whispering to each other and laughing. You could tell it was put on so everyone else thought they were having such a great time. I found it disconcerting. On the other side to me was a woman. She was stunning. Tanned skin and tousled brown hair tied loosely in a bun on top of her head. I could almost imagine other women walking past her in the street and secretly calling her names because of her hair. She had an amazing tattoo of Ganesh that covered almost the entirety of her back. Aviator glasses, cigarette hanging loosely from her lips and the yoga pose completed the look and instantly made me fall in love with her.

I slipped into the pool unnoticed. Not that I was trying to be secretive, but no one seemed to care what I was doing. The water was the perfect antidote to the Thai sunshine. My skin cooled in seconds and I slowly drifted to the bottom. Despite the years upon years of smoking I could still hold my breath for a good ninety seconds without too much trouble. I looked up through the water and could see the beautiful hippy girl sitting in her meditation pose. With the way the water moved she had the appearance of being in some sort of dream state. Maybe I was dreaming. I didn't want to wake up if I was.

When my lungs felt like they were going to burst through my chest I pushed myself back up and treaded water for a few minutes just my eyes and nose breaking the water. I watched her meditate. She seemed to be hardly breathing. I couldn't take my eyes off of her. My mind worked overtime trying to think of a good reason to strike a conversation. Even to know her name and where she came from would be enough.

Sitting on the edge of my lounger I lit a cigarette and laid back enjoying the sun. I pulled my sunglasses on and let the sun's rays dry my skin. It's a great feeling having the sun warm your skin back up after the coldness of the water.

'You want a drink?'

I opened my eyes and squinted. Even with glasses on the Thai sun hurt.

'Please, I'll take a bottle of beers.' I couldn't see who I was speaking to.

'Food?'

'Maybe later. Thank you.'

The shadow disappeared from view. I hadn't known that drinks were served around the pool. This hostel was getting better. A few moments later I heard the bottles being placed next to me and then opened. I didn't open my eyes again and instead just said thank you. The rude couple walked by whispering and laughing. I didn't like them but wasn't going to let them spoil my peace. Fuck them, I enjoyed the sun and the Marlboro.

'Hey.' It was the cute girl from across the pool. 'Hey, are you staying here?'

I tried to play it cool and sat up slowly as if it were the first time, I had realised her presence. I took a long hit from the beer. It was so cold that I hiccupped. Not quite the impression I wanted to give off.

'Me?' I said.

She looked around the now empty pool. 'Unless you can see anyone I can't?'

She was Swedish. Or maybe Danish. I feigned looking as well. 'Yeah right. I got here late last night. You?'

She stood and started towards me. She was more beautiful than I first thought. She moved with such grace but with a definite sultry edge that would make some men come in their pants.

'About a week ago. I'm heading up to some of the hill tribes tomorrow.'

'Jesus, why?'

'What do you mean?'

'Nothing.'

She sat on the bed opposite me crossing her legs. Perfect skin up close. 'Where are you planning on going to next?' She untied her hair and let it fall to her shoulders.

'Laos. I want to ride an elephant.' I sounded like an imbecile.

She crinkled her nose and looked for an out. I'd seen it a thousand times. 'Ok. Cool. Do you know which one you will visit?'

'Which elephant?' I laughed. 'I don't know any personally.' Oddly, she laughed with me.

'You are strange and funny.' She took the cigarette I was about to light and flicked into her mouth.

I sipped my beer and hiccupped again. I was about to launch the bottle into Burma when she smiled gently and slid it from my fingers. Her index finger lingered long enough on the back of hand to nearly get me hard. She was intoxicating.

'I'm Ruben by the way.'

She took a long seductively slow mouthful of beer. Her eyes constantly on mine. I could almost feel her running around inside my head. Her eyes were a sparkling light brown and held me willing me to take a leap of faith into them. If I did, I feared I'd never come back.

'Freja.' She finally said.

She handed me back the bottle. I lit a cigarette. Not because I particularly wanted one, but I needed something to do with my hands.

'So, Ruben let's start again. Do you know which sanctuary you want to visit?'

'What do you mean? I was just going to book one when I get there.'

'Well, none of them are totally ethical but some are better than others.'

'Did you know in Bangkok they walk baby elephants in the busy streets?' I said.

'It's truly horrible isn't it, Ruben? Why would they treat such a graceful animal in such a way.'

We sat in silence for a few minutes. I guess she was genuinely considering the plight of those poor creatures. I thought of her naked. Then I realised my bottle was empty and started looking round for whoever it was that had brought me the last one. Finally, a head appeared at a window on the other side of the pool. I couldn't tell if it was a man or woman from where I was sitting. The floating head shouted something at me to which I replied by holding the empty bottle up and making a V sign.

She finally woke from her daydream and stubbed her cigarette out. 'Come.' She said standing.

'Where? I've just ordered two beers.'

'My room. I have flyers for some of the more elephant friendly places in Laos.'

I looked towards the window of the floating heads. 'Shall we wait for the drinks?'

'We can get them on the way. Come. I have weed.'

I almost pushed her in the pool making my, towards the window.

CHAPTER 15.

I stepped into her room the same way you step into a sectioned off part of a church or museum. For the first few steps I kept expecting someone to jump out, hit me over the head and drag me to the alley round the back.

She was laying, face down rummaging through pieces of paper she had collected along the way. I wouldn't describe them as flyers. More secondary school dance leaflets. I could see her swimming bottoms through her sarong. Her arse was perfect.

I leant against the dresser slightly unsure of where my place was. I looked round. Her room was a shit hole. There were clothes and empty bottles everywhere. It made me feel a little, nauseas.

'Here it is.' She suddenly said.

'Cheers. And this one is more elephant friendly?' I didn't give a fuck to be honest but needed to keep up the pretence of caring.

'Totally. Pass me a beer please.'

'So, did you want me to roll then?' I said.

She walked on her knees across the bed to where I stood and grabbed my t-shirt. I stumbled forward and she kissed me. I cupped my hands against her face and pulled her closer. Her skin was so soft. I opened my eyes and looked for her moisturiser. I hadn't noticed any before.

She gently pulled away. 'Not yet.' She whispered. 'Weed is in my bag over there.' She pointed to the side table. 'I'm going to take a shower. I hate smelling of chlorine.'

I watched as her sarong dropped to the floor and she stepped into the shower room and as she closed the door, she gave me the subtlest of winks. I wanted to marry her there and then.

Rolling the joint, I paced the room and had a look through her stuff. She had been to quite a few places according to the leaflets she had acquired. I tossed them to one side and slouched onto the bed lighting up. I inhaled deeply, holding the smoke in. It was good strong weed. I had another look in her bag and snuck a bud or two into my pocket for later. Moving a ridiculously small pair of white pants I found the ashtray and reasted the joint on the side. I held the pants up to the window examining them and flicked them across the room. I doubt she'd have noticed. She lived like a homeless person.

After five minutes I was getting bored of staring at the shower door. How did she have such soft skin if she spent this much time in the shower. I could hear her singing and thought about joining her, but she had said "not yet". Did that mean we weren't going to have sex today. She was leaving in the morning so what was the point of me being here. The weed had started to take over my reasoning and the paranoia begun to set in. I couldn't take the walls staring at me anymore so went for more beers. I heard the shower switch off as the doors slammed on my arse.

Opening the door with my elbow I kicked the bottom a bit harder than I meant and it swung open.

'Jesus Ruben.'

'I went for beers.'

'And you came back a Policeman.' She laughed. I didn't get it.

She was sat on the bed in a pair of Muay Thai shorts and an old Ramones t-shirt. Her hair was left down and was still wet but not soaking. She looked incredibly sexy. I almost threw the bottles to the floor and stripped. The baggy shorts showed just enough leg to tease your imagination. And she certainly pulled them off better than most of the other morons that wore them out here that thought because they wore the shorts that made them professional fighters and were routinely having their skulls pummelled by actual Muay Thai boxers.

'What are you reading?' I put the bottles on the side. She was still drinking her first one.

'Raymond Carver. You read him?'

'Yeah of course. What language is that in?'

She looked at the front cover as if she had forgot what country she was from. 'Danish.'

'I didn't know they printed him in Danish.'

'Why? Have you been checking?'

'Um. No. I suppose not.' I felt stupid.

'Sit next to me.' She patted the bed. 'But bring me another bottle. This one has gone warm. And the ashtray.'

Draining the last of the warm bottle she took the top of the next and set it on the bedside drawers. I lit the joint and passed it to her.

'So, you like Raymond Carver?' She asked.

She took two long drags and passed the joint back to me. I took one and threw it into the ashtray.

'Yeah.' I thought I had already said that. 'Do you have any music? I feel like I haven't listened to any since I left England. Except The Beatles.'

'No, sorry. I don't.' She sipped her beer. 'So, do you have a favourite Carver book?'

'Fuck no. To be honest I've always preferred John Fante or Bukowski.'

'I never liked Bukowski. He is too rude. Too brash.'

We spent the next few hours discussing which author should be granted the title of "Best Author". She put up Wolff and Carver. I stuck with Fante and Bukowski. When we bored of that subject, we moved onto why The Stones were better than The Who. And how the Americans invented Rock and Roll, but the British showed them how to do it properly. The whole time we smoked and drank. I went for more when the bottles ran dry. I never once thought of having sex.

I checked my watch. It was almost ten. I was shattered and Freja was fast asleep. I stood and steadied myself on the side of the bed. Pulling a cover over her I kissed the top of her head. Sex had never been on the table with her. I realised that as I watched her breath heavily. She simply wanted some company. Someone to pass a few hours with. Closing the door on that extremely beautiful Viking it dawned on me that when you're travelling on your own. It's not about getting from one city or town to the next. It was all about going from one companion to another. It's about meeting as many people as you can to make the long periods you will have to keep your own company that bit more bearable. And if you need to pretend that you want to have sex with someone to make that happen then so be it.

I rested my head back and folded my hands behind the pillow. I was happy and not just because I was stoned and drunk. I had a sense of wellbeing that I hadn't felt in a while. The idea of getting to Luang Prabang now excited me. Who I might meet didn't scare me as it once would have. I had had an epiphany. I could still see the actual getting there part being fucking tedious though.

Reaching into my pocket I pulled out my wallet and took out Charlie's number. I had considered calling a few times since I had been out here. Mainly to tell her I was doing the travels like we had spoken about. But also, to just hear her voice again. Then I thought of Charlotte. If I met her again it would be a minor miracle. I had no idea where she was or even if she was still in Thailand. I was just about to cross into another country so it would be reasonable to think that she had already left this very strange intoxicating place.

I turned the small yellowing piece of paper over and over be-tween my fingers. I flicked my lighter and set the corner on fire. Lighting a cigarette from the flame I tossed the burning paper into the ashtray. Living in the past wasn't helping me and I needed to move on. I watched her burn away into memory. I had loved her once. I probably always would.

CHAPTER 16.

The bus journey from Chiang Mai to the border town of Chiang Khong took me through Chiang Rai. I had stopped the night there and can honestly say the place depressed me. I'm sure there are nice parts. I just didn't see them. By the time I stepped off the bus I had had enough of anywhere that started with Chiang. Unfortunately, I had the night to wait before I could cross into Laos.

Chiang Khong is not a huge town. Mainly used by tourists to stay a night or two before they jump the border. I had checked into a simple hut. Double bed, side table and an electric fan to blow the warm air around. The bathroom was through the back, no door required. The toilet had obviously been green at some point in its life. Now it had a brownish yellow glow about it.

Sitting on the plastic chair that had been left on the veranda I swung the spare one round and put my feet up. My watch said half five in the pm. The sun had started to drop behind me. I reached down and pulled a bottle of beer and a packet of crisps from the 7/11 bag. The beer was nice and chilled. The crisps were shit. As I lit my pre-rolled joint the sun cast huge shadows of the trees that stretched all the way down to the river.

The mighty Mekong River. I had seen so many war movies over the years that talked about this river and read dozens of books that gave the Mekong as mythical a status as the Nile or the Amazon. Here I was getting ready to cross it into lands unknown. At least unknown to anyone in my family. I felt like Caesar staring across the English Channel not knowing what or who were waiting for me on the other side. I had overheard a few people in Chiang Mai say it was nothing like Thailand. Laos was and still is essentially a Communist state. If a true communist country still exists. Even China is basically just another America but without proper elections or any form of human rights.

I rested the joint on the ashtray and sipped the beer watching fishermen bringing their boats in and tying them to wooden stakes. There was hardly a sound other than a feint din from a far-off bar. It was truly peaceful. After the events of the last year, I needed some peace. Some quiet time. My life had almost evaporated, and I was lucky to be here. Charlie was now in the past. She didn't need me, and I didn't need her to survive. I re-lit the joint and inhaled heavily throwing it back after. Looking up I noticed bats flying between the trees searching for insects. I exhaled the smoke and took a long deep breath. I could handle this pace of life. I think it would suit me.

I hadn't left a letter for Charlotte at the last hotel. It would seem needy and very pathetic leaving them at every stop I thought. I'd had this romantic idea that she would eventually meet me somewhere down the line and she would run into my arms crying and confess her undying love for me and how my letters had helped get her through the lonely nights and long journeys. She had probably had sex with the first Australian she had met in the horrible hostel that she was staying in and forgotten all about me. Who knew. The letters would be opened in a few years by a night receptionist who have a good laugh at the stupid, scared westerner.

Finishing the first beer I resigned myself to the idea this was the best way to go. On my own, meeting new people along the beaten path. Maybe I would bump into someone to fuck a lonely night or two away with. If I didn't then so be it.

I flicked open a copy of "Ask the Dust" and opened another beer. The sun had fully set.

CHAPTER 17.

Here I stood on the banks of one of the world's great rivers ready to conquer another country. Standing with hands on hips and my bag on the floor beside me I couldn't see the boat I had been promised would be waiting for me.

'There, there.' She pointed upriver.

'Where?'

'Silly boy. There.' She put a little more effort into the pointing.

I could see a small dot in the distance coming from the Laos side. 'Great.' I said.

She had insisted on coming down and waiting with me despite my protests against the idea. It was her brothers' boat, and she was bringing him breakfast. The parcel being clutched tightly to her stomach didn't appear to have food inside. It would be hard to get open with all that duct tape around it.

I had considered turning down her offer to arrange the crossing and going to the actual "port" up the road. That was until she told me it would be free with her brother. I had shaken her hand and paid what I owed for the room.

'What the fuck is that?'

'Boat. Take you to Laos.'

'That's not a boat.'

She looked up and down the full two meters of its length. 'Boat.' She said again slightly confused of what I had said. She pointed again just to hammer home what she was referencing.

'No, a boat keeps water out. It is the fundamental part of its design. This has almost as much inside as the river has.'

The young man driving the boat had no clue what I was saying. He just smiled and carried on bailing out water with the bottom of a large plastic container.

'Ok. You get in and he take you across.'

I thought of walking away and going to the proper crossing, but it was a free ride and I had wasted too much time waiting here. All the other boats would probably be fully booked by now. I looked across the river. It could only be a few hundred metres. Worst comes to worst we would sink half-way and I'd swim the rest of the way. The only thing I had to worry about was my passport and money getting wet.

'Do you have a plastic bag and some tape?'

She looked at me blankly, her brother just smiled and continued to shovel water from the half-submerged husk. I acted out me putting my prized possessions into a bag and taping the top. She got the idea straight away and produced a sealable zip tied bag from her pocket. It wasn't an everyday item you would carry. Especially all the way out here. I didn't want to know why she had it so gratefully took it and closed my passport and money inside.

Once I had climbed into the boat I relaxed. The old lady passed her brother his lunch and we pushed off. I sort of already knew it was drugs but really didn't want to think too much about it. With my bag on my lap, we started towards the eastern shoreline. I lit a cigarette and tried to enjoy the short journey and take in some of the scenery. The water in the boat didn't appear to have gotten much deeper as we neared the middle, so I forgot about having to swim and took out my baguette the old lady had handed me while we waited for the boat. I was trying to work out what the filling was when the driver reached across and snatched the roll away from me.

'My lunch.' I think he said as he bit into the bread.

I leant forward on my bag and smoked my cigarette. The diesel fumes from the engine made me feel sick.

We were baring down on the banks of Laos before I had had time to finish smoking. I tossed the butt into the bottom of the boat. As he killed the engine we slowed and drifted towards the shore and the bottom instantly filled with ten inches of water. I could see the panic on the drivers face as he frantically tried to scoop out the water before we sank. I sat very still hoping to hit the bank before the inevitable happened. Around fifteen feet from land his bailing out turned into shear frenzy and lost all sense of coordination. He was just splashing the water against the side rather than tossing it over the edge. The water was now somewhere between my ankles and knees depending which way the waves hit us. I thought of jumping overboard but had no idea of the depth. I quickly calculated that at the rate he bailed compared to the water coming in we should just make it before getting too wet.

Two feet from safety and he had given in to nature and we were both standing on the seats. The boat now three quarters full. Actually, it was no longer fair to consider it a boat but more driftwood. He didn't look too bothered by the situation we now found ourselves in. He just stood stoically smoking a weird roll up ready to go down with his ship.

We stepped onto dry earth as the boat jammed into the mud of the bank. The rim of the edge just about showing above the water line as the Mekong claimed another victory. I shook his hand and thanked him for the lift. He nodded and smiled. Asking him which way I had to go he simply shrugged and walked away leaving me standing there before he disappeared through the bushes, parcel in hand.

I passed through passport control having paid for my visa and followed the throng of white faces into a restaurant where a Laotian man stood at the front holding court. He was rambling on about how long the boat journey would take to Luang Prabang. I listened to two Kiwi girls behind me talking about how they had heard horror stories of the horrendous town that everybody stayed in half-way. I didn't fancy it and thought about going back to Thailand.

'There is another option.' The man at the front said suddenly. Holding a finger in the air it grabbed my attention.

I raised my hand. 'How long and how much?' I shouted.

His eyes brightened and fixed on me. 'It will take no more than six hours the boat is twenty.'

'How much?'

'Cheap. To you for being first just twenty Dollars.'

There were a few murmurs but generally everyone stayed still. Not daring to be the first to break ranks from the others. I jumped to my feet and marched to the front desk and slammed a twenty-dollar bill down. 'Sign me up for the short route please.' The young pretty girl behind the desk just slide the money out of sight with a very beautiful smile and pointed outside.

CHAPTER 18.

I sat on the side of the road smoking a cigarette when every-one started filing out of the restaurant. It was like a scene from Shindlers List. People carrying some form of luggage dutifully keeping in line and being herded to fuck knows where. All you needed were some Alsatians and men with guns. More fool them, I was taking the quick route and would be enjoying a glass of beer by teatime while these suckers would still be on a stinking boat in the middle of nowhere. I unfolded the map of Laos that I had taken from the front desk. Finding where I was now, I tried to locate Luang Prabang.

I had always been good with maps. My Saturday job growing up had basically involved guiding my Dad around the Kent and Essex countryside looking for the new building site he would be starting on. It was great times. Just me and him listening to The Beautiful South and eating ice lollies in the summer and hot pasties in the winter. I would have to call him when I reached my destination. This was the longest I'd gone without speaking to him or my Mum. I missed them both.

I traced my finger along the main roads I guessed we would have to take. It looked a lot more than six hours driving. I tried to find a shorter route. There were mountains of some sort in the middle and the only way seemed to take us almost all the way to the Chinese border.

'Hey, I thought you said it would only take six hours?'

'No. I said it should only take around six hours. Maybe more but maybe less.'

'You definitely said only'. I over emphasised the only part. 'In fact, that was the main selling point.'

'My English not good. You mistake not me.'

'Fuck off. You were Oxford educated half an hour ago.'

He smiled and drank from a bottle of water. He was smartly dressed in shirt and chinos and obviously well-schooled in taking tourists money. 'It's up to you. Can take the boat with the others or you can take the ride I've arranged.' He nodded behind me.

I turned around expecting to see a rusty piece of shit to be trundling down the road spewing black smoke out. Instead, the minivan coming my way appeared almost brand new. It eased to a stop in front of the salesman. The white paint shone in the morning sun. The door opened and I could instantly small fresh leather and a hell of a lot of air-freshener. I peered inside the seats looked comfortable. The air-conditioning was blasting away. There were even small TVs in the back of the front seats.

'They work?' I said pointing them out to the shady fucker stood next to me.

'For five extra dollars, yes.'

I didn't answer him back as the driver caught my eye. He was grinning at me like an idiot would at their own reflection. I took it that this was possibly the first time he had driven a brand new car like this.

'You still want the boat? It's not too late.'

'No this will do I suppose.'

I chucked my bag into the back climbed in and settled into one of the quite luxurious seats and waited for the journey to begin. After twenty odd minutes I'd got bored and went for some travel snacks and a bottle of whiskey.

'Are we leaving anytime soon?' I said getting back in.

The driver gave almost no reaction other than to shuffle in

his seat. Another half an hour past and he suddenly started the engine. This was it we were on our way to the promised land of Luang Prabang. We didn't move and five minutes later he switched the engine off again. I tried to see the salesman, but he had disappeared taking my money and my remaining faith in humanity. I had finished the snacks and started on the whiskey. It wasn't the best but at this moment in time I would have drunk petrol.

'Sorry.' I tapped the driver on the shoulder. 'Are we leaving or is this Luang Prabang? Did I fall asleep?' I laughed at my own joke. I wanted to cry. The driver got out and lent against the side of the van.

I drank some more and leaned out of the van to smoke a cigarette. Flicking the butt into the side of the road I closed my eyes to the morning sun. It was nearly eleven.

The passenger door opened, and a youngish woman got in holding a large white box. It took me completely by surprise. She didn't speak to the driver and ignored me as if I weren't in the back seat. She seemed very strange. Without warning the salesman appeared and slammed the door on me. The driver engaged first gear and the van shot down the unmade road. He crunched through the gears until we hit tarmac. I eased back into the seat and enjoyed the scenery racing past my blacked out windows. Laos seemed beautiful once out of the dusty town. Fields rolled into one another dotted with palm trees and the odd house thrown in with seemingly no reason for them being there. I dozed on and off. The gentle rumbling of the tyres on the road was always my nemesis. Any sort of white noise killed me. My mum had told me once that when I was a screaming baby, she would turn the hoover on and I would instantly calm. As I grew up, when the dreams became too much to ignore and the alcohol stopped working, I would turn a hairdryer on and lay next to it positioning the end to blow the air across my ears. The combination of the white noise and the warm air would silence the voices and dreams and allow me to sleep.

The driver slammed the brakes on startling me back into the real world. A cow or ox, I couldn't tell which, had decided to take a nap in the road. I checked my watch. It was four o'clock. I'd been out for nearly four hours. Getting the drivers attention after he finished wiping the sweat from his forehead, I asked how much longer we had. By rights we should have nearly been there.

'Yes, yes.' He said.

'Excuse me.' I tried the woman instead. 'Do you know how much longer we have to Luang Prabang?'

'Long time.' That's all she had for me.

I settled back into the seat and stared through the window. We were somewhere in the mountains. I think they were mountains. I'm not an expert. We seemed very high up and the drops off the side of the road were long enough that you wouldn't be very well if you fell off.

I took a long drink of whiskey to clear the sleep from my head and tried not to think of the certain death should the driver swerve the wrong way the next time some livestock wandered into the road.

'Hey. Can I smoke in here?'

No answer.

'Can you ask him if it's ok for me to smoke in here while we're driving?'

'No.'

'What no I can't or no you won't ask him?'

'No.' She replied.

Fuck you I thought and lit up opening the window at the same time.

'No smoke. The driver said no smoke.'

'Sorry? I don't speak your language. And you didn't ask him

anything.'

I defiantly carried on smoking.

'You want him to pull over and leave you here?'

'I beg your pardon?'

'You be dead in ten minutes.'

I thought for a second and tossed the cigarette out of the window.

'Good choice for you. We stop in one hour.'

'Is this your van or something?'

'No.' We went back to one syllable answers.

By the time we pulled of the road it was getting close to half five and the sun was thinking of going into full retreat. Where we had stopped wasn't so much a service stop as it was more a dirt patch and an area of jungle cleared to act as a toilet. There wasn't even a shop to buy food. It was disappointing to say the least.

I took a piss in the toilet clearing, always one eye on the tree line. I wasn't sure what would come out. A tiger. Maybe a rabid monkey or a Vietnam vet who still thought the war was raging. As I came back through the bushes that had been very well trimmed to give a slight modicum of privacy a nice orderly queue has started to form. The man next in line looked in pain and was clutching a handful of paper. I walked back towards the waiting vehicle happy in the knowledge that I wasn't following him.

The driver was resting against the side of the van smoking. I joined him and pulled the map from my pocket and spread it out across the bonnet. I found Luang Prabang and motioned to the driver with my finger and a hopeful smile a few centimetres above. He returned my smile and pushed my index closer to the Chinese border. I felt deflated and tried to work out how much longer we had. Judging by how far we had come, about an index finger's length in five odd hours. To how far we had left, the ring finger's length. I estimated another six or so hours at least. So much for the six hours all in promise.

Leaning back, I noticed just how beautiful my surroundings were. There was a hazing mist that had settled across the mountain tops which looked as though it stretched all the way back to Bangkok. The sound of monkeys echoed through the ravines. I looked over the edge but couldn't see the bottom due to the thickness of the canopy. If I believed in paradise, then this could just be it. This could be that perfect moment in time when nothing else in the world matters and it would last forever. And obviously if people weren't shitting in the bushes a hundred yards away would help. I guess this would be how we would treat paradise should it be an actual place.

I managed to squeeze in a few cigarettes and a quarter of the whiskey before the strange elusive woman came back from God knows where. She had probably been slaughtering children in the village down the road and smearing their blood over her torso.

'We leave now.' She barked slamming her door.

The driver threw away his cigarette leaped into his seat and started the engine in a blind panic. He had only just lit another up. I relaxed enjoying the rest of mine and watched his slowly burn away in the dirt. Eventually her head came through the open window and she glared at me. She didn't speak. She didn't have to; her eyes tore any resilience I had away. Terrified of what she may do to me I joined the driver in hastily jumping back inside. We set out before I could close the door.

There wasn't much conversation to be had so I didn't try and since they had relented and let me smoke, I left them in peace. One village we had to slow down to pass through seemed to be having some kind of dance. A petrol tanker ahead was struggling up the hill, so we were barley moving. As we pulled alongside what came across as the village hall, we all looked through the open doors to see what could only have been the entire population dancing around a box of beer Lao. The adults all had a bottle in hand and smiles on their faces. I caught the woman's face in the side mirror. She was smiling too.

'Been to many of those?' I said. 'Looks like fun.'

'Not for a while.' She turned away. There was a sense of morose to her.

I passed the whiskey forward and she took the bottle and put down a long hit before handing it to the driver. He declined thankfully and slid it back to me.

'Thank you.' She said.

'I'm getting out. It'll be quicker to walk.'

I lit up and walked alongside the van as it struggled to keep a steady pace behind the almost stationary tanker. Some men came towards me carrying another box of beer, so I approached them and asked to buy a couple of bottles. None had a clue what I had said until my travel companions shouted at them through the window. The man carrying the box offered it to his friend who took two bottles out and handed them to me while making the official money gesture.

I turned to the van. 'How much do I give them?'

She closed the window ignoring me. I pulled some notes out and handed the man five Dollars. He stared at the money in his hand and then at his friends. They all laughed and gave him a congratulatory slap on the back. They handed me a bottle opener turned and walked away in the direction of the party. They all seemed very happy with the deal. I opened one of the beers and stepped back into the waiting vehicle. It had hardly moved since I got out.

'How much you pay them? They look happy.'

'Five Dollars. He even gave me the opener.'

She laughed and said something to the driver. I heard Dollars.

He laughed. I wanted everyone to stop laughing.

'That why they happy. Foreigners. You have no idea what you do.'

I swigged the beer. It was good. I didn't want to converse with them anymore. I had had enough. My arse hurt from all the sitting down. She passed me a cigarette. I took it and rested my head back. By the time I had finished the first beer we were out of the town and heading downhill away from the highlands. I wanted to ring my mum. She would have appreciated the view from the toilet stop.

I don't remember falling asleep. I suppose you never really remember the actual point you become unconscious. The dream was as vivid when I woke as it had been when I was asleep. They always were. Most people have a bad dream and by the time they have finished their first coffee or toast the memory had faded to nothing more than a mere footnote. For me, the nightmare stayed all day. Sometimes that day became plural. As a teenager I would go days without showering due the memory of what I had dreamt. It's one of the reasons I don't bath. The feeling of being vulnerable. I couldn't look into mirrors for fear of what may be staring back at me. For weeks on end my life became a perpetual nightmare.

Charlie was there again. This time it was different though. She was calm and at peace. We sat on a beach my head in her lap as she stroked my hair. The waves gently lapped on the shore. I could hear a baby crying but couldn't turn my head no matter how much I tried. Charlie held my head down. I started crying and panicking. I knew the sea was carrying the baby out but there was nothing I could do to stop it. She just kept telling me it would be ok.

I screamed out when I woke. It was dark and I was in the van on my own. I couldn't tell if I had woken inside another dream. That was another beautiful trick my mind played on me. Tricking me into thinking I was awake when really, I was still fucked.

Sweat was dripping off me. I was soaked through. Stepping out I lit up as the driver came out of a small wooden building eating. He smiled and got back in.

'How much longer?' I said leaning inside.

'One hour.'

'Fuck. Really.'

He nodded and started the engine. I checked my watch. It was just after nine. I walked to the back of the van and took a piss against the wheel. As I finished, I noticed her watching me.

'Come we make good time. Luang Prabang by ten.' She moved passed me. 'You sick boy. Too many demons in your head.' I didn't know what she had heard me say in my sleep, so I didn't respond.

We pulled away sharply and the woman's white box slid from her footwell and hit my toes. I was about to kick it back when the box moved.

'What the fuck is in the box?' I said.

No one answered so I reached down and lifted the lid. Something tried to bite me, and I pulled my hand quickly away. Reaching down again I slowly moved the lid across. I was sweating. Inside were some turtles or could have been tortoises I could never tell the difference. These little fuckers had proper beaks and looked very nasty. Lifting the box carefully I passed it forward to her.

'You should not look.' She snapped. 'Not your business.'

'Well fuck you then. You shouldn't smuggle animals.'

I didn't care so much that she was obviously smuggling these things, but I did care that she was doing it with me in the car as well. I had no idea of the sentence that this would carry if she were caught. It was a guarantee I would end up with some of the blame. The drugs on the boat were different. He was clearly well versed in it.

The talk again was non-existent for the rest of the journey. All I can say was cigarettes were smoked and beer and whiskey were drunk. If they had been smuggling drugs they would have been taken too.

CHAPTER 19.

We arrived in Luang Prabang a little before ten. It was Sunday night and it felt like it. The place was like a fucking ghost town. There weren't even many dogs roaming the streets. The strange woman had gotten out on the outskirts of the city and jumped into a waiting car but not before threatening to find me should I mention to anyone about the boxed animals. I wanted to call my dad to come and get me. When the driver dropped me off in the middle of a large square, he threw my bag into the kerb, waved, and left.

I sat on my bag in the darkness for a few minutes trying to get my bearings. Everything looked closed. I had to find somewhere to sleep quickly. I had tried to be more spontaneous this time and hadn't booked anywhere in advance. The first four places I tried told me "tomorrow". The next two just said "no". I wandered around for a bit not really knowing what to do until I noticed some lights on at the end of an alleyway. There were English speaking voices drifting towards me.

'Hey.' I said. 'Do you know if they have any rooms available?'

There were four of them sat around a small coffee table drinking beer and smoking weed. They looked at each other for a few seconds longer than they should have. I felt uncomfortable. Why didn't I just pre-book. One of the men gave an annoying chuckle. The type that you instantly know is going to bring bad news and make you feel stupid.

'Man.' I hated him already. 'You obv's don't know that the festival only finished yesterday.'

He was American or Canadian.

'Festival?'

'Yeah man. No one is going to be moving for a couple of days at least.'

'I have no idea what you're going on about.' I looked to his companions for some sort of help. They were all very stoned. One of the girls answered this time. She sounded Spanish. I was very tired.

'It means you will be very lucky to find a free room until tomorrow. I would try to take a taxi bike. You will get round the hostels faster and they may know somewhere with rooms.'

I thanked her and quickly made my way back to the square where the van had left me and found a few men standing around a strange motorbike come trailer taxi.

'I need a room.'

'Yes.'

'Yes. I need a room. You take me?'

'Yes.'

He didn't move so I gestured towards the taxi. 'Come on then.'

I had to give the driver his due's. He stuck with me when most would have robbed me and dumped me by the side of the road. After another hour of "no's" and "tomorrows" we sat in the back of the trailer together and smoked a couple of cigarettes and shared a bottle of beer. We were brothers in arms by this point on a quest for the elusive grail. I knew there was an airport nearby and kept that as a last resort for bench sleeping. It would be near deserted at this time of night so a safer bet than the middle of town.

'I go home soon.' He said making a sleep motion with his hands.

'I come with you?' I was only half joking. I don't know why I had started using pidgin English.

He laughed. His broken teeth looking like bombed houses. I couldn't believe I had just shared a bottle with him. I almost retched.

'No.'

He didn't say another word except to ask for payment. I gave him some notes and he climbed onto his bike. Before he pulled away, he pointed in the direction of a large building, the lights were blazing away.

'Western hotel. Lots of rooms.' He drove away.

I looked at the building and back at my taxi disappearing into the blackness. 'You fucking prick.' I shouted after his shadow.

We had driven past the hotel a dozen times and he hadn't mentioned the little fact that it was a hotel. And a fucking large one at that. I had been perfectly played. Again. As I walked the few hundred meters to the entrance it dawned on me why Daisy had told me to take the travel guidebook and why Charlotte insisted on having one. Even Bernie the marshmallow man treated his like the scriptures. Fuck come to think of it Lauren didn't put hers down in Rome. I wished I hadn't left mine at Heathrow. I probably wouldn't buy another one but at least I could see the point of them now.

Pushing open the main doors a young man sprung from his chair behind the reception desk and stood to attention.

'Good evening sir. How may I help you?'

'At ease soldier. I need a room please. Or the use of that very comfortable looking couch over there.'

I don't think he understood the first or last part of that sentence, but he did happily tap away on the hidden keyboard.

'Yes sir. I have one room available.'

'Done. I'll take it.' I wanted to kiss him.

'The room rate is one hundred and fifty Dollars per night including breakfast.'

I would have paid two hundred had he asked.

'Is there a mini bar?'

'Of course, sir.'

'Then which way?'

Not ten minutes later I was sat in a warm bath surrounded by floating empty miniature bottles. It wasn't a bad way to end a truly awful day. I could see the very cosy looking bed, inviting me in. I was grateful this day was almost at an end. I wouldn't be moving on for a while now. Or at least till morning.

I climbed in bed and pulled the duvet over my head. I fell asleep. Well, I think I did.

CHAPTER 20.

After the night in luxury, I found a hostel down overlooking the Mekong. It seemed cheap enough at fifteen dollars a night. The bed wasn't very comfortable, but it was clean. I had my own shower and toilet which was a bonus compared to some of the other rooms I had looked at in a similar price range. I couldn't bring myself to have to share the basic facilities with strangers. The only problem with the room was the fact that it always felt damp. It didn't matter what time of day or night it was there was always enough moisture in the room to drown a small child. It could have been the time of year or its close proximity to the river, but I just couldn't work out why it was so bad. I would like to have seen how they would have spun it in The Lonely Planet guide. "Great location, cheap and you get your own bathroom. The only downside to this hostel is your clothes, bedding, bags or just generally anything that can absorb water will be fucking saturated the entire time you are in the city". Not quite the punchy hook line they'd be hoping for.

There is a claim that Luang Prabang has the best baguettes outside of France. It's a tradition that goes back to the colonial days of France in Asia. Always seems strange when you mention the words colonial and a country that wasn't raped by Britain. That's right we weren't the only bastards out here. I've never been to France and have no real desire to so I'm saying that the baguettes in Laos are the best in the world. Even better than Upper Crust at London Bridge.

I spent my days lost in this old city walking the back streets and wandered along beside the river. I would find a café on the rivers banks and eat baguette sandwiches and drink the famous Beer Lao. I read and smoked and enjoyed being by myself. When I finished a book, I simply went to one of the shops off the main square and traded it for another. I had everything here that I needed. No one bothered me or wanted me for anything. It was a peaceful existence. Even being damp stopped getting to me after a few days.

I had walked past the entrance to a particular monastery a few times and had told myself "next time" whenever I thought of going in. You see the monastery in question was at the top of a very steep set of stairs. I would stand at the bottom looking up until the steps disappeared into the trees, cigarette dangling from my lips thinking "I'll get you next time. Maybe after some lunch".

On one day. I think it was a Thursday but could easily have not been. I was stood staring down the barrel. I had just put the cigarette out and was about to walk away when a Laos lady who appeared to be around eighty tapped me on the arm.

'The more you look, the more you won't do.'

'I'm sorry?'

'You will be.'

She then marched past me and set off up the stairs. I had to follow. Striding past her I gave her a smile and she laughed shaking her head. It wasn't a well done laugh. It was more of you moron you're going to die. I ignored it anyway and pushed on. In my head I was the great Edmund Hillary, and she was my Tenzing Norgay. The heavy breathing started around thirty steps up. By fifty I thought I was going to black out. Maybe it was altitude sickness kicking in. I persevered and around halfway I had lost count of the steps and collapsed into a heap almost blocking everyone else's way to the top. A very helpful Kiwi told me to get out of the fucking way. I called him a cunt which he luckily chose to ignore. I was in not fit state to do anything other than die.

I sat on the steps and smoked a couple of Marlboros to kick start my lungs. The views even from here were quite amazing. I noticed my stand in Norgay heading towards me with her toothy grin. She gave me a reassuring squeeze of the shoulder as she went past, and the image of her wobbly arse is the last I have of her. Imagine if Norgay had left Hillary like that and claimed the glory for himself. Would have made a better story.

I pushed myself to my feet and powered on like only a true Brit can and made the summit. I felt elated. It was like being Bobby Moore, Churchill and Rocky all rolled into one. I was a certified hero. The view was out of this world. One side was the river and jungle as far as you could see. The other was mountains in the distance. I know I'm not quite selling it but trust me if Hilton could they would knock the fucking temple down and slap a five star spa resort up there and charge people a hundred dollars for a toe rub.

Time seemed to stand still up there. Monks roamed around between tourists not paying too much attention to the constant snapping of cameras. I sat and watched one young monk gracefully move past some kneeling golden statues and perch himself on top of some stones and stare out at the mountains. I watched him for around ten minutes. He didn't move a muscle. I wondered what a young boy like him could have to think about that would keep his mind so occupied for that amount of time. I could barely stretch a thought out for more than thirty seconds.

A woman approached him and said something. I couldn't hear what she had asked the boy so moved a little closer. The monk shifted his weight, so he turned away from her without seeming rude. She pulled a camera from her bag and started clicking away at him. He moved again so the woman side stepped around to photograph his face. The young man put his hand up in protest. She ignored the not so subtle hint and continued her assault.

'Excuse me? Sorry.' I said.

'What?'

She seemed lovely already.

'I really don't think the young fellow likes having his photo taken. Maybe you should leave him alone.'

She tried to ignore me and put the lens to her eye again. I covered the front of the camera with my book.

'What the hell do you think you are doing?' She was pissed off.

'I'm trying to tell you in the nicest possible way to stop.'

'What has it got to do with you?'

'Nothing really but it isn't very nice. He's only a kid.'

'So, he shouldn't put himself on display.'

'Don't be so fucking stupid. He has come here to meditate not be photographed by you. You would have to be English as well wouldn't you.'

'What is that supposed to mean?'

I really wanted to slap this woman. Old enough to know better and not as high class as she would have you believe. I put her somewhere in the home counties, but not Surrey or the expensive part of Berkshire. Given her white lace ups and trousers that failed in their attempt to make her chubby ankles I had to sadly say Kent.

'I mean of all the countries in the world that people here are from the only one acting a cunt has to be English. And southern no less.'

She gasped in total shock. I may have been a little too harsh. Putting the camera back in her bag her hand trembled. 'Well. I have never been spoken...' Her voice trailed off.

I took a long drag on the butt I had forgotten I was holding and blew the smoke over her head. The young monk stared at both of us. I wasn't sure if he understood nor cared what was happening on his behalf. One of her friends joined the party. She was dressed the same. Even had the same tight haircut. They looked as though they had slept in rollers like my nan used to. It made me laugh a little.

'Everything ok dear.'

'No. This horrible young… I can't even bring myself…'

'Your friend was being very rude to this boy.' I said.

Her friend looked me up and down then started to lead her friend away.

'He looks like a bloody beatnik.' She said.

They stopped a few feet away and turned back to me. 'You are the cunt young man. Your mother would be ashamed of you.'

I didn't know what to say and just laughed out loud. They left. I turned in time to see the monk vanish around the opposite corner. Little shit didn't even have the curtesy to say thank you for defending him.

Sitting on the rocks where the boy had just been, I stared at the mountains. I couldn't understand the vow of celibacy but could see why they chose this life. It made the material hungry ideals we value so highly just seem stupid. I found a comfortable position and relaxed. I had nowhere else to be and no one who needed anything from me. I could have happily shaved my head worn the shit orange robes and spent the next few years sat up here on this rock pretending to ignore the tourists.

After about an hour I was hungry and wanted a cigarette so climbed down lit up and went to find somewhere I could buy a baguette. I checked my watch as I descended the steps. I had managed an entire one and a half hours up there before leaving. Maybe a monk's life wasn't for me, but it was definitely an option for the future.

CHAPTER 21.

I had seen her a few times over the past week or so. Luang Prabang wasn't the biggest of cities and you found yourself bumping into the same faces and having that awkward shall I or shan't I say hello moment. I tried to ignore most of them. Especially the ones with the big expensive cameras and the "fuck you I'm rich and on a gap year" expression plastered all over their faces. Those one's could all get dysentery for all I care.

She was different though. We used the same restaurant for breakfast. I would sit pushing my French toast around the plate and watch her play with the local kids. She seemed to be able to speak their language which I found amazing. I could never get a table close enough to her to be able to listen to what she spoke to the kids about. They seemed to adore her. In fact, oddly I had never even managed to get a proper look at her face. It was always a fleeting glance. The restaurant was a popular hangout and unless you were there early you were resigned to the back near the toilets. There were always too many people obscuring my view at the exact moment she came into eye line. Instead, I would sit and play with my food and invent the idea of what she looked like and how our first conversation would play out. That was another serious problem I had had since childhood. It had hindered me through quite a lot of my life. In almost all aspects in general day to day living where I would need to speak to anyone from a job interview to simply ordering a coffee, I would try to go through how I thought the conversation would go. Constantly trying to guess how the other person would react or respond to what I had said or did. It was fucking exhausting. If ever there was going to be more than one person in the exchange my brain would feel like it was going to pop, and I'd come close to a stroke.

I was trying to cut down on smoking. After being shown up by an old lady in a crushed velvet tracksuit walking up some stairs, I had decided to give my lungs a bit of a break. Instead of smoking the cigarette I rolled it between my thumb and forefinger. Occasionally I would try to flick it into my mouth like I'd seen so many of the old Hollywood stars do in the films my Dad made me watch. I had only managed to achieve it a few times. Most often than not the cigarette would bounce off my nose or completely miss me all together and land on the floor. I bent down and picked up the cigarette after another failed attempt and noticed she was no longer in her usual position on the steps leading into the restaurant. I stood up far too quickly for the time of day and instantly had a rush of blood to the head. Steadying myself I tried to find her in the crowd.

'No worry. She back tomorrow same as you.'

'I'm sorry?' I turned to the waitress beside me.

'You watch pretty girl. We watch you.'

'It's not like that. She...' I trailed off. She what? I had nothing.

'I bring you beer. Maybe she come for lunch.' She walked away but not before taking the cigarette from my hand. 'Floor dirty. Smoke another.'

I walked out onto the street and lit up blowing the smoke to the mountains. Fuck I was beginning to get lonely. Romanticizing over someone who I had never met or even seen fully was a new low point for me. I needed to leave town and move on. Luang Prabang had been great but I was growing stale here. Keep moving Daisy had said. I stubbed the butt out in a plant pot and looked across the road to a sign advertising an elephant sanctuary. I thought back to the poor creature I'd seen in Bangkok and to Charlotte. I wondered what she was doing and who she had met. I should have left another letter in case she had come through the same route as me. Maybe I should just head straight back to Bangkok and try to find her.

I went across the road and booked a ticket to the sanctuary. The tour took in a waterfall as well. It was touted as the most beautiful in Northern Laos. The bus didn't leave for an hour, so I had time to drink the beer that had been offered in the restaurant.

There was a leaflet under the bottle from the company that produced the beer. I read it while I waited for the waitress to come over and take the cap off. I had nothing else to read as my book had come to an unceremonious end the day before when on page two hundred, I turned to realise that the last person to read the book had blacked out every other line on the next forty odd pages. I had been fuming and thrown the book in the bin. The leaflet in question had some colourful photos of the Laos countryside and a remarkable claim that drinking beer was safer and better for you than drinking water. It told the reader that you should give your children beer in small quantities rather than the contaminated local water supply. It may not have had the children part but that's how I remember it. To be fair when I showered, I kept my mouth closed and head turned away from the water and would definitely choose the beer over water. I just found it strange as to why they would print these flyers in English when even the inexperienced travellers knew that drinking local water was the equivalent of buying ecstasy from a bloke called Nigel in a pub car park.

Tossing the paper on the table I closed my eyes and wondered what all the doubters would think of me now. Here I was in the middle of Asia fending for myself and not a care in the world. I was in the same mould as the great British explorers who had gone out and conquered the world before me. So, the majority of it wasn't our finest hour in history but at least we didn't try to massacre everyone like the Belgians did in the Congo. There is a country with small man syndrome. Never really gave the world anything except how to capitulate and the massively over-stated sense of one's self-worth.

'Do you mind if I steal a smoke?'

I opened my eyes. 'Charlotte. Fuck me.'

'Not yet Ruben but I am happy to see you.'

I was flustered. I jumped to my feet almost too quickly and hugged her. 'What are you doing here? How did you know I was in Luang Prabang?'

She lit the cigarette and sat down putting one foot up on a spare chair. The sun had been kind to her. Freckles had started to appear on her nose and under her eyes. Her hair was loosely tied in a bunch on top of her head like this was the way it had always been. With her Aviators tucked in the neck of her t-shirt and the new fuck you attitude that oozed from her she could have passed for a foreign war journalist taking some downtime from the Vietnam war.

'So, when did you get here?'

She scanned the restaurant and signalled to the waitress for a beer. She was different from the plane.

'I arrived yesterday. Came in via the boat. It was an amazing trip.'

'I bet it was.'

'What do you mean?'

The waitress winked at me as she opened the bottle. I ignored it.

'Sorry?' I said.

'What did you mean "I bet it was"?' She sipped the cold beer. 'How did you get here if you didn't take the boat?'

She was a lot hotter than when she had left me in Bangkok. I didn't want to tell her the truth. 'I'll have to show you the temple up on the hill if we get a chance.'

'Ruben.'

'Yeah.'

'How did you get here if you didn't take the boat?'

'Took a cab.'

She laughed. Then she took a large gulp of her drink and laughed some more. She didn't appear to be slowing down so I lit a Marlboro while I waited for her to stop.

'Was the taxi ride enjoyable?'

She was mocking me. 'It was actually. I got to see the mountains up near the Chinese border.'

I wanted to keep the moment of paradise to myself. If I told someone else about it, even Charlotte, I feared it would be ruined. It happens all the time. You find a restaurant you like or a hotel that no one has been to before. Even a piece of music that you think is the best thing you've heard since the last great song you listened to. Then you stupidly tell someone. They take it upon themselves to test your theory and delight in shitting all over it and don't hesitate in telling you why the food was awful, and the hotel was full of wankers. And oh yeah, the music was a rip off of an old song they had already heard and preferred.

She half stubbed out the cigarette, so the smoke still drifted up into my face. People not putting their cigarettes out fully really aggravated me. I reached across and finished the job.

'So, what have you been doing here? How long have you been in Prabang?'

'Prabang? Not much really. I've done a lot of reading. Been to see a few temples. Just really chilled out to be honest.'

She took a look around the restaurant and finished her drink. 'This is nice here.' She finally said.

'Do you want to come and see the elephants with me?' The question blurted out. I wish it hadn't.

'Are you sure I won't be imposing?'

'I'd love the company. It's ok being on your own for a little while.'

She stood pushing the chair back loudly. 'Wait here and I'll nip across the road and book on. I take it that's what you were doing over there.'

I watched as she left. There was something about her that made me feel differently. I wasn't ashamed to be vulnerable around her. I didn't need to build the walls up when I was with her. You could squeeze the amount of time I had actually spent with Charlotte into a short weekend, but she made me feel calm as if the black fog was lifting. I still had the perpetual feeling of loneliness but that had been with me since birth. I could be anywhere surrounded by family and friends and I would have the deep sense of a nagging voice telling me that these people were better off without me. It doesn't matter how well your life is going. If you can't shake the idea that you don't deserve to be loved, then you're fucked. When Charlotte looked at me. When she spoke to me. I honestly believed that she wanted to be in that moment with me. That she actually wanted to hear what I had to say. With Charlie she was always trying to be somewhere else. Whether that was through the drugs and alcohol or simply just fucking off at a moment's notice, but it meant I still felt alone when I was with her. I understand that she did what she did because she was a prostitute trying desperately to escape the clutches of her controlling pimp. I tried to make it work. Offered her a way but she rejected me. Pushed me away. I could have moved to Scotland with her or at least Newcastle but she didn't want me.

'Right, I've booked on. We leave in twenty so get your shit together Ruben.'

I hadn't noticed Charlotte come back in. Charlie was still an all-consuming force in me.

'Yeah, I'm ready.'

CHAPTER 22.

The ride out to the elephant sanctuary was great. Charlotte had a portable CD player, and we shared the little in ear headphones. People across the world had started downloading music to little devices that fit comfortably into your pocket and didn't need to carry caseloads of CD's around with them. I could never see it catching on so stuck to the vinyl's and CD's. They were a bit like touch screen phones. Who the fuck wanted one of those? She had managed to get her hands on a copy of a Jimi Hendrix mix of songs in Bangkok. Staring through the window of the minibus to the Laos countryside listening to "Crosstown Traffic" and "Little Miss Strange" I was transported back to the late sixties and could almost have been a GI on the way to an outpost ready to fight the VC. I tried to imagine what it would have been like. Never having left the town you were born and raised in to suddenly be in the middle of the jungle with a Vietnamese soldier armed to the teeth and running at you screaming in a pair of flip flops. I wouldn't have known whether to throw my arms in the air and cry or fall on the floor laughing at how absurd it all was.

Charlotte stroked my arm. 'You ok?'

'Me. Yeah. I'm great, why?' Better than I've been in a while I wanted to say.

'You were miles away.'

'Decades you mean.'

She didn't answer that. Pulling the sunglasses down from her hair she placed them gently on the bridge of her nose to deflect the bright sunshine that had suddenly come out from behind some clouds. I watched her for a few seconds as she mouthed along to "All Along the Watch Tower". She seemed to know the words. To the verses as well as the chorus. I let my eyes move down her body and stared at the small butterfly tattoo on the inside of her wrist. It was delicate and beautiful like Charlotte.

I went back to watching the countryside flash by. What I had seen of Laos so far was stunningly beautiful. I doubt I would have given my life for the place, but it was nice. I turned back to Charlotte. She had an unlit cigarette dangling from her lips and was flicking through the leaflet of the sanctuary. She was a graceful hippy sent from the past to capture my soul. I didn't want to be apart from her again but knew it would happen at some point soon and we'd end up going in different directions. I also hated the idea that she may have read the letters I had left. They would come up sooner or later. Even if she did not mention them the thought of not knowing would drive the wedge between us. I had to know. Maybe she had read them and thought they were a romantic gesture. Maybe she thought I was a cunt.

I reached across and took the cigarette from her and tossed it into my mouth catching it perfectly between my lips. I thought I heard her say "cool". 'Yes I am.' I said. She took the cigarette back and carried on singing along. I leant across and kissed her on the cheek. She smiled, held my hand, and kissed me back on the lips. She had my soul and could do whatever she wanted to with it.

CHAPTER 23.

'So, what do you think?'

'Of what?'

'The waterfall. It's beautiful isn't it?'

'It's ok.'

'That's a slight understatement Ruben. It's perfect.'

'There the problem lies.'

'Pardon?'

'It's too perfect. Look at the rocks over there.' She looked at the rocks that were peaking just enough through the flowing water the create an almost picture perfect ripple of white foamy water. She turned back to me, arms in the air. 'They were obviously positioned there.' I finished.

'Oh, fuck off Ruben. You're only saying that because that arsehole at the sanctuary told you it was manmade.' She had a point. 'You would never have had a clue if he hadn't filled your head with shit.'

'I'm just saying it's a bit suspect is all.'

'Well lets go to the top and have a look.' She laughed and kicked water at me. 'You never know we may find a tap.'

The elephant sanctuary had been ok. If I'm honest after the ride on one of them, which only lasted fifteen minutes, I had become a little bored. There wasn't really anything else to do. I wasn't sure what I had been expecting. Maybe something a bit more than just standing around waiting for your turn to feed the elephants who were too old or unwell to carry fat tourists up and down all day.

The ride itself had been amazing. You were taken down through the jungle and along the middle of the river. It just didn't last long enough. It was long enough to realise that elephants are hairy buggers and not at all comfortable.

I left Charlotte waiting patiently in line for her turn at feeding them and went to find the smoking area. You weren't allowed to smoke near the elephants as they didn't like the smell or something, so you had to go and stand in the corner like the peado in the group. I got talking to an older couple from Milton Keynes and had mistakenly told them that we were heading to the waterfall afterwards.

'What's funny?' One of them, Gerry I think his name was chuckling.

'Oh, nothing dear. We were there yesterday. Got this very nice young man to drive us out there.'

'Gerry. I do wish you would stop telling everyone this story.'

'Shut up Peter. They have a right to know what they're spending their money on.'

'Yeah Peter. It's my money.' I took a mouthful of the Beer Lao I had bought from the kiosk.

'It is all a fake you see my dear.' Gerry continued. 'The whole fucking waterfall is manmade.' He said this with one hand cupping the side of his mouth as if someone in ear shot may actually care.

'Fuck off.'

Peter tutted his disapproval and walked away. He had clearly heard this story re-told a thousand times in the last twenty-four hours.

'I kid you not. The area is far too well manicured, too uniformed. And I should know.'

'Why?'

'Why what?'

'Why should you know? Because you're gay?'

'Oh no darling, I'm sorry I should have said. I'm a town planner.' Gerry threw this statement out there like he had planned the entire city of Bath all by himself. He even straightened the collar on his flowery shirt. This man could have been the twin of Wayne Sleep.

'Right. Do you work on many waterfalls then?'

'Well, no but I did plan one of the more difficult interchanges in Milton Keynes. It's one of the reasons we moved there.'

I suddenly had the real desire to run after Peter or even queue up with Charlotte and the other loonies. I glazed over as he regaled me with the pitfalls to planning a busy working crossing. I wanted an elephant to rampage and trample me to death. Or not even to death just maim me enough for this pain to stop.

'So, do you have any proof the waterfall is manmade?' I had to cut him off before my ears began to bleed.

'Proof.' He was taken aback that I didn't take his immediate word for fact. 'The proof is clearly evident when you get there my boy.'

'So, that's a flat no then.'

'That is a definite no.' Peter said returning with three fresh beers. I gratefully took one.

We spent the next twenty minutes or so enjoying the cold beers on offer and chatting about where we had been before this. They had travelled a lot since they met in London during the eighties. They were a genuinely nice couple.

'So, who is she? Girlfriend?'

'Who?'

'Who he says' Gerry looked at Peter who just smiled. 'The

young very pretty girl you haven't taken your eyes off for the last half an hour.'

'Charlotte.' She still had at least ten people in front of her. 'I hope one day.'

Peter leaned closer. 'She's very beautiful.'

I knew that already and didn't answer. I just watched her waiting, dried corn cob in hand. I wanted to go to her and hold her hand. Nothing more at this moment. Just to be close to her. She turned and looked at me and grinned holding the cob in the air. I was in trouble. I said my goodbyes to Peter and Gerry and walked to where she still patiently waited.

'Shall we get going?' I said. 'Looks like you'll have heat stroke before you get to feed them.'

'Yeah, fuck 'em. I don't think they'll starve.'

On the way to the waterfall Charlotte and I shared a cigarette and she put "Exile on Main Street" on her CD player. As we drove through the jungle, she rested her head on my shoulder and dozed. I could smell her hair. Even after a morning in the hot sun she still had an amazing aroma.

CHAPTER 24.

'Come on Ruben. What's the matter with you?'

I waved my hand for her to carry on without me. The heat was getting to me no matter how cool the water was. I sat on one of the rocks and let the water cover my legs to the knee. It was instantly relaxing. I watched the other people who had come to the waterfall that day. None of them seemed to care if it was fake or not. They were simply happy to be here in this beautiful place. I tilted my head and stared up though the overhanging trees to the blue sky beyond. I had to find out if it was real or not. The water was just too clear to be natural.

'Ruben. For fuck sake will you get a move on. My nan is faster than you and she has arthritis in her hips.'

'I'm coming.' I took one last look at the sky. I don't know what I was looking for. Maybe some sort of sign that showed me I was where I should be.

We reached the top of the falls. When I say the top, we're not talking Niagara, or the Victoria falls here. The top was just up a slight incline. It was a hill that someone in a wheelchair could manage even if they had to push themselves. Charlotte stood hands on hips searching the bushes beyond. There was a small river that flowed into the falls.

'There you go Ruben. There is your tap.'

I moved further up and pushed some of the bushes aside. The most anyone could be accused of was artificially widening the river to create the waterfall. Turning back to Charlotte I came to the opinion that it really didn't matter anymore. The area was beautiful, and people came to enjoy it. If someone somewhere had this idea, then good luck to them they made people happy.

'Told you. You shouldn't be so cynical Ruben.'

'You're not the first person to tell me that.'

'Can we just enjoy the rest of the day then? This place is perfect.'

She had such joy and enthusiasm in her voice that I didn't have the heart to point out the large blue pipes that I had just noticed to the left and right of the river a little further upstream pumping water in and speeding the flow up. They could have been to clear standing water from up the hill. Or connected to a pump somewhere. Watching her knee deep in the clear cool water, hands behind her head facing the sun I would have been a cruel person to expose even the slightest chance of foul play. Sometimes ignorance is bliss and even nature needs a little help every now and again.

CHAPTER 25.

'So, what are your plans?'

I was pushing scrambled eggs around the plate and watching out for the mysterious woman to arrive. She hadn't been in for a couple of days now. She must have moved on.

'Ruben?'

'Yes.'

'What are you planning on doing next? You've been here a while, now haven't you?'

I nodded. I wasn't sure how long exactly I had been in Luang Prabang, but it was definitely time to be moving on.

'So where next?'

Too many questions. 'Not sure. I've heard of a place called Vang Vieng. Supposedly you float down a river on a huge inner tube and stop at bars all the way along.' I put my fork down bored of the eggs. 'Could be fun.' I finished.

'Sounds good. I'm thinking of heading to somewhere called Don Det. There are around four thousand islands there.'

She was reading from her guidebook. I watched how intense she studied the words on the page. Her lips moved very subtly when she read, and she twisted her hair around her fingers.

'Why don't you come to Vang Vieng with me first. We could go to the other place after.'

She smoothed the pages flat before closing the book and pulled a cigarette from my packet. 'I don't know.' She lit up turning the lighter in her fingers. 'I really want to spend some time on the islands before I cross back into Thailand.'

'Ok, we'll go to there, first then.'

She took a long drag from the Marlboro. There was an awkward look on her face, and she wouldn't meet my eyes. The waitress brought two beers over and set them down in front of us. I checked my watch. It was eleven and past the yard arm somewhere in the world. Charlotte sipped hers first.

'Listen Ruben. I've really enjoyed the last few days...'

She let the words trail off. 'But?'

'But I want to go on my own. That was always the plan when I first booked my flights.'

'Right.' I was devastated. 'Yeah, it's probably best anyway.' I downed half the bottle and signalled for another. 'So, when do you leave?'

'In the morning.'

'Fucking hell. I suppose you don't want to waste any time hanging around here.'

'It's not like that Ruben. I just don't want to get bogged down in one place for too long.' She smoked trying to find the right thing to say to the obsessive weirdo sat in front of her. 'I never planned on meeting you at the airport but now I have.'

'Yep.' I cut in. 'Don't worry yourself about it. You don't have to explain.' I smiled and nodded. I don't know why I nodded. It just happened but made no sense.

The waitress came across and was removing the caps when I slammed down the empty bottle. 'Just keep them coming.' I picked up the next and instantly started.

'Ruben getting pissed in here isn't going to change anything. I'm just saying that we should still travel to the places where we had planned to rather than simply following each other around.'

I knew she was right. Deep down. Very deep, but all I could see at that moment was that just like everyone before her she was fucking off and leaving me to it.

'Seriously. It's good. You go to this place with all the islands, and I'll stay bogged down here.'

'Fuck you Ruben.' She sat and anger smoked her way to the butt while very aggressively drinking her beer. 'Listen I'm hoping to be in Thailand in a couple of weeks. What do you say?'

'I'll see. I might like this Vang Vieng and stay there a while.' I was heartbroken. I didn't want to her to leave me again. I drank the second bottle in one and waved it in the direction of the bar holding two fingers up. The waitress hurriedly brought them over and opened them. I felt bad for being an arsehole to the waitress.

Charlotte pushed her chair back and stood up. She walked the two whole steps to me and crouched down so that she had to look up at me. 'There is a place called Lonely Beach on Koh Chang. I should be there by the end of the month like I said. Meet me there. Please Ruben.'

I sank the third while keeping eye contact. I wanted so much for her to tell me she was joking and wasn't really leaving. The last few days had been amazing. We had walked together by the river and sat in cafes just reading. No need for conversation. Talking of the life we had left behind in England seemed to be pointless. Trivial. This was all that mattered in this moment in time. We kissed as you see in the movies with a passion and yearning for these days to last forever. It was just the two of us and the mighty Mekong river. No world outside this city existed.

'I'm not sure. Like I said Vang Vieng. It has a river with bars along the banks and big inflatable wheels. Who wouldn't like that?'

'You wouldn't.' She straightened up. 'Lonely Beach. End of the month. She bent down and kissed me on the forehead. Her lips were warm and soft. 'Be careful Mr Humphrey.'

I watched her leave. All five feet something of perfectness. My head screaming for me to go after her and apologise for being so fucking childish. I couldn't move. The tears rolled down my cheeks. I was an idiot.

'Don't cry like baby. You scare customers.' I looked up. The owner stood next to me. 'Drink this. It make, you man again. You think pretty girl like you cry like baby.' She slid a bottle of whiskey in front of me.

'Fuck off.' I lit a cigarette and took a long slow hit straight from the bottle.

'Hey.' She pulled the bottle down spilling some on the table. 'Use glass. Fucking animals drink in street.'

CHAPTER 26.

I stumbled around my room kicking empty bottles out of the way. Thirty minutes until my bus left for Vang Vieng and I couldn't find my shoes. I was now four days into this binge and had had a total of around two and a half consecutive hours sleep in that span of time. There had been sleep on other occasions, but I had only managed that amount of time in one sitting. I found a bottle with half left in the corner next to the bathroom. It was placed neatly in a line of empties against the wall. I couldn't see where the cap was. Picking the bottle up I slid as gently as I could down the wall and drank. It would be the second bus in as many days I had missed if I didn't find my shoes.

The shower was dripping onto a towel. I didn't remember putting the towel there, but the dripping had obviously annoyed me at some point. I stank. I could smell myself without having to bend my neck. My teeth hadn't seen the brush since I'd let Charlotte leave. I did try a couple of times, but as soon as the bristles went past my first molar I gagged and threw up. Letting the bottle roll across the tiles I crawled to the shower, reached up and turned the hose on. It was basically a garden hose with a normal shower head jammed into the end. The cold water soaked me instantly and after a minute I just felt stupid and cold. I changed my trousers, but not my shirt. On the way out I picked up my bag and walked barefoot to the bus pick up point a few streets away.

I needn't have worried about missing the bus. The driver was still loading bags ten minutes after we were due to leave. I fell into the last available seat. There were a few other travellers on the bus but mainly the clientele was local Laotians. The bus carried on past Vang Vieng all the way to Vientiane the capital. I rested my head on the glass, it was beautifully cold and eased the headache that had started to form behind my eyes. I longed for the bus to move so I could try and fall asleep. They said it would take around five hours to get there. As long as I could sleep, I didn't care.

The engine started, doors slammed, and we set off heading out of town towards the road south. I relaxed almost immediately. It was an old bus, so the engine made the whole vehicle vibrate and hum. I started dozing. My head like a nodding dog I kept butting the seat in front so gave up fighting it and rested back against the cool glass again. Sleep came quickly and I was grateful for it.

I woke. I say this hesitantly as it took at least a minute or two for me to realise I wasn't still inside a dream. I have no idea how long I had slept for. It felt like seconds. We have all had that sleep where you are so tired and drained that a mere blink lasts for several hours. I didn't feel refreshed in any way. The bus was virtually empty except for one of the men who had some sort of job with the running of the vehicle. I had seen him playing with the engine before we had left. I made my way past him to the exit doors and noticed a Kalashnikov rifle under his open jacket. I paid no more than a glance as I still wasn't sure I was even awake. Stepping off the sun hurt my eyes even through my sunglasses.

'Which way to the toilet?'

The driver thumbed towards the queue of people. There were a dozen of other coaches all lined up alongside mine. I went to the back of the bus and joined another man urinating into the wheel arch. This man also had a gun. A handgun of sorts.

'Why the gun?' I said nodding towards the American style holster.

He patted the handle with his piss covered hand. 'Bandits.' He said casting his eyes across the landscape. My gaze followed his. I had never seen a proper bandit before. I didn't think they even still existed. Were there men and women in the jungle waiting to pounce on anyone who veered too close to the tree line? Or did they drive up alongside the busses and climb the sides like something out of MadMax.

'Where are they?'

'Watching. Always watching.'

He made another theatrical sweep of the hills. I zipped up and moved away from him. He'd be the first to get it should the elusive bandits come steaming through the tree line. The food stall smelt great.

'What's that?'

'Chicken noodle soup. You want?'

'Yes please. And two beers.' It might not have been chicken, but it smelled and look good. 'Hey, is that real Vat69?'

'Yes.'

'I'll take that too. How much?'

'You pay Kip or Dollar?'

'Whatever is easiest. I'll give you twenty Dollars.'

'Ok. Deal.'

She almost ripped my hand off for the note. The whiskey was probably fake, so I decided to wait until I was back on the bus before I tried it. I could see a hundred miles of jungle in every direction I could be buried in for making a scene here.

'I'm taking a pair of these sandals as well.' She didn't flinch so I found my size and put them on. Made from a basic type of plastic they were surprisingly comfortable. I'd seen hundreds of people wearing them and I didn't want to continue barefoot.

Taking my noodles, beer, and whiskey I found a tree trunk to sit on. The noodles were very tasty and spicy without being too hot. I topped up my drunkenness with the beers and sat for the brief time I had enjoying watching this busy service stop going about its daily business as it had done for years before I had stumbled across it.

As a child I used to struggle to comprehend how other areas of the country could be carrying on their lives when I wasn't there. It wasn't an ego trip that I was the centre of the universe or anything. I just could not see past my parents and me and the area I was growing up in. When I was around seven or eight, I honestly believed that when we left a town or city that wasn't home everything stopped and would have to wait for me to return before they could carry on.

I chain smoked three cigarettes with the driver before boarding the bus. He was a really nice guy. Told me he had family living in America and that he hoped to have enough money saved soon to take his own family out there. I took it he meant to stay rather than visit Disneyworld for two weeks and come back to drive the bus through bandit country.

CHAPTER 27.

'Hi, do you have a room?

'Yeah.'

'Ok, can I see it.'

'Yeah.'

This was becoming hard work. He just stood staring into nothingness. 'Can we look now?'

'Yeah sure. Take a seat over there and I'll get it ready.'

'Cheers.' He was obviously very stoned. 'Where are you from?'

'Sorry? I'm from here.'

You could barely see his eyes where they were so screwed up. 'You're not from Laos. And you have an English accent.'

'Dude don't fixate on where people are from. In the end we are all from the same place.'

'Well, that's clearly not true. I'll be over there then.'

Slipping my sandals off I climbed the small steps that led up to the raised seating area and sat in the corner. There were two other people around my age deep in conversation. They didn't look up or acknowledge my presence. I rested against the wall and lit up. The bus had dumped me in the middle of town and when it had disappeared, and the dust had settled this was the first place I had seen. It seemed clean and quiet from the outside. There was another place a few doors down, but they had dance music pumping through the open doors and windows.

I picked up the menu card from the small table next to me.

I was still struggling to get to grips with having to sit on the floor in some of the restaurants. I found it an uncomfortable way to eat. I kept getting indigestion. I did however like the custom of removing your shoes whenever you went inside a shop or place to eat. It made things seem cleaner. They served the usual baguettes and soups here and standard selection of beers. I couldn't see French toast. This would normally be a deal breaker, but I was too tired to look for somewhere else and could always just ask them to make it.

'Hey.' One of the other two was looking at me. His friend was also reading the menu.

'Hey.' I replied.

'Where have come from?'

'Luang Prabang. You?'

'We just came up from Don Det. You heard of it? We're heading up to Luang Prabang next.'

I'd heard of Don fucking Det. 'Yeah it rings a bell.'

'I'm Mike and this is Fred.' Fred still didn't look up.

'Nice to meet you. Ruben.' I pulled the bottle of whiskey out and had a drink. There didn't appear to be anyone taking orders. 'So, what's his deal?'

Mike laughed. 'Who Billy? He's a bit fucking strange. Live's in the back room through there with his transexual partner. You'll meet him or is it her? Fuck I don't know anymore. He calls her Lizzie. She is very nice.' He took a large gulp of the beer he had. 'If he isn't stoned on Yabba, he's shooting Heroin into his arms. He's a fucking mess.'

'I thought he was stoned.'

'That's nothing mate, yesterday he walked through here stark bollock naked with Lizzie who was also naked. I thought Fred here was going to have to excuse himself to the toilet.'

I laughed as Fred finally looked up from the menu. 'What the fuck Mike. It's confusing. From the waist up you have this beautiful woman with stunning tits and then you look down to this set of cock and balls.' Fred rubbed his eyes and pushed his hair back. 'Man, I need to go somewhere with a bit of normality.'

'What's Luang Prabang like Ruben?'

I thought for a second and stubbed out my cigarette. 'Normal.'

The room was lovely. White walls, very comfortable bed. Billy had apologised that he only had a room with en-suite, so it was a little more expensive. I was happy to pay more not to have to share toilets with someone I had said. The window looked out over the main road to the left and also a small garden below. I could see the top of someone's head sitting on a bench, a cloud of smoke rising up. I presumed it to be Billy's girlfriend. The bathroom had an actual electric shower. I left my bag by the front door. There was a chest of drawers, but I didn't see the point of unpacking. It had been made crystal clear that while it was ok to smoke in the room it wasn't ok to smoke in bed. There had been a fire a couple of years ago and someone had died. I filled a glass with the last of the Vat 69 and spent the next ten minutes walking between the bathroom and the front door. There was no real reason for this other than to kill time.

I had a shower. It was the first proper wash since Kanchanaburi where I had a constant stream of hot water which I let cover my face for a few seconds until I needed to breathe again. Turning I tilted my head to the floor so the warm water could run across both my ears at the same time. I couldn't hear anything other than the running water. It gave me the detachment from the world I needed to be able to think.

I stared at my reflection. My skin had browned, and my beard had grown long and out of control. My hair was now past my ears and starting to lighten from the dark brown it had always been. I moved away from the mirror before I saw something, I wasn't comfortable with.

Laying back naked on the bed I put the ashtray on my bare

chest and lit up a cigarette. I needed a drink but was just too exhausted to go downstairs to the bar. I finished what was left in the glass from before the shower. Watching a very large cockroach come through the open window I dozed. The shower had relaxed me. I stubbed the cigarette out.

CHAPTER 28.

'French toast and a Beer Lao, please?'

'You want beer with breakfast?'

'Yes please.'

I had slept for almost twenty hours straight. Mike told me when I first came back down that Billy had panicked when no one had seen me the previous evening. He thought I had come, checked in and drunk myself to death. One of the girls who work in the restaurant had been sent up to check on me. I felt great. I couldn't remember the last time I had slept for more than a few hours in one night. As I waited for my brunch to arrive enjoying my first smoke of the day life seemed good again. I sort of wished Charlotte hadn't shown up before. My head was clearer when I was on my own and she had mixed things up. Maybe I was better off without women in general.

I checked my wallet. Money was becoming a problem. I'd have to change a traveller's cheque soon. Looking at Billy he was shot to pieces. His eyes were like piss holes in the snow.

'Billy.'

'Yeah. Who want's something?' This guy was completely fucked. He turned in circles like a tourist on the underground.

'Billy, this way.'

'Oh, Ruben it's you. What's up dude? I thought you was dead last night. The girl I sent up was shocked. Said you were completely naked.'

'I heard. I need a bank. I'm running low.'

He went back into a daze. I couldn't tell if he was thinking of the nearest bank or had drifted into a catatonic state. 'Billy mate. For fuck sake.'

'Yeah. Top of the head I'd say out and turn left. It's at the end of the road.'

He made a weak gestured point off to the right. I'd ask someone else as he was obviously out of his mind.

The French toast was good. Even though it wasn't on the menu they seemed only happy to make it. I used the syrup this time and actually enjoyed it. I was never a lover of syrup. Whole time I ate I could not take my eyes from a blackboard to the left of the front security roller shutter. It had around half a dozen names written on it. Mine had been added to the bottom. Some had ticks next to them while the others had crosses. The ones with ticks had been crossed out as well. It was like a very public death match. I pondered what this could mean. It was pointless asking Billy as he wouldn't remember his own name. Luckily, Fred came down. He was only wearing swimming shorts which I found weird.

'Fred. Hi. Why is there a board with everyone's name written on it? And more importantly why are some crossed out?'

'No one explained the board yet?'

'No.'

'Ok, it's simple. Old druggy boy over there is supposed to close the shutters on the front at eleven. The only problem with that is firstly everyone would tell him to fuck off and just bang on them until he let them in. And second for him to close anything would involve him not smoking himself into oblivion or injecting shit into his arm.' We both looked at Billy. Resting his head on the counter. 'Poor wanker barely makes it through the morning without smoking Yabba. Someone a while back came up with this idea, so everyone wins. Everyone staying here has their name on the board. You put a tick next to your name if you're going out for the night and cross if not. You get me?'

'Yeah, go on.'

'He pulls the shutter down to a few feet from the floor just before nine when he is getting ready to jack up in his little den of Sodom. Everyone coming in after this crosses their name through and the last person in shuts them all the way down.'

'Simple.' I said.

'Except for the one prick the other night who crossed everyone's name off, closed the shutter and went to bed.'

I laughed. It sounded like something I would have done.

'He went fucking mad. Threatened to start closing at nine for good.'

'So, do you know anything about him? Other than he clearly needs help.'

'You mean how comes a posh boy from the West Country ended up in the middle of Laos' one and only party town running a hostel?'

'Pretty much?'

'One word. Heroin. Supposedly he came here a few years back and got trapped by the lifestyle and the easy access to smack. I spoke to someone here a couple of days ago who said there is a rumour that his dad is quite a high up priest or something.'

'No shit.' I said.

'I think it started going downhill for him when he would take a beer or two with breakfast.' He winked at me and excused himself.

I folded the last piece of toast in half and dipped it in the syrup. Wedging the entire slice into my mouth the sticky juice poured from the sides of my lips. I wiped it away with the back of my hand and drank some beer to wash the eggy bread down. Billy rocked gently back and forth behind his counter. Just another poor soul trapped by not being able to let go and plagued by what his life could have been. They were all over Asia. Men and women in the slightly too far past it stages of life trying to cling on to something that should have been past the next generation. Or even the next next generation. Laughing at my own cynicism something struck me. I couldn't remember how long I had been in Laos. My visa was only for thirty days and I'd heard they didn't take kindly to over stayers. I'd have to check my passport stamp when I finished breakfast. I ordered another beer and a shot of whiskey. I felt better, but I wasn't ready to stop drinking.

CHAPTER 29.

I floated down the middle of the river on my four Dollar tractor inner tube. The bars on either side were ok in themselves but came across as a little forced. By the time I had reached the third one the constant screaming of excitable girls had started to aggravate me. And the young men jostling for position to show how cool they were by swinging from ropes into the river became annoying. There were too many people and coupled with the body paint and ridiculously loud dance music I had had enough. Instead, I bought a bottle of whiskey from the bar and a packet of cigarettes, jumped into the tube, and pushed myself off.

Floating on my own was like being a viewer of a reality show. I would gently stop in front of a bar and just watch everyone jumping around and dancing. I'd stop for a few minutes and maybe enjoy a smoke and a couple of slugs of whiskey. When I bored of the frolics I would simply paddle away for the next show. It was quite nice. The hills rose up either side and I would imagine myself as a member of the SBS secretly observing the enemy positions before I had to call in air strikes. I would hold a pretend laser sight on the bars that had the biggest looking arseholes and call in the warplanes through my imaginary walkie talkie.

I reached a bend in the river that had bars opposite each other. I couldn't decide which one I would have destroyed by a cruise missile. They were equally annoying, but I only had time to wipe one out before the enemy spotted me. I watched a girl in her mid-thirties vomiting into the river while a younger man no older that twenty groped her tits from behind. When she finished, she swilled a beer round and started kissing him. I held up the laser and called in the co-ordinates.

'Hey dude? You want to come to this bar. The one over there is full of losers.'

I had stayed in this position too long and had been compromised. I paddled myself round to face the enemy guard. He was younger than me, but not by much. The American accent and long hair said surfer.

'I'm fine, thanks. Probably just going to keep going.'

'Come on. We have all the beers. Our bar is way better than that one.'

I looked past him. There were three people sat around sharing a joint. I turned my head back to the other bar. I quickly counted at least sixty people. 'I'd say their bar is wining. You have all the beers because no one is there to buy them.'

'I have Yabba.'

He held onto the side of the tube. 'Not interested. Like I said I'm moving down the river.'

'Come on man. Just fucking come in man.' He started to sound a little too aggressive and was clearly wired.

'I think you need to fuck off and let go.'

I pushed myself away from him.

'Just come and have a beer man.'

'I would do, but you all look like a bunch of cunts.'

I gave my arms a huge push to take myself further away as he splashed about in a rage. He shouted something in my direction, but I couldn't hear through the dance music from the bar I had just destroyed. Floating once again on my own I didn't come across anymore bars. Instead, I took in the tranquil stillness on the hills and river. I had one more day before I had to leave Laos, and this seemed a great way to spend it. Tickets on the overnight train to Bangkok were booked and all I had to do was reach the Thai-Lao Friendly Bridge on the other side of Vientiane. I lay back into the tube and roasted in the sun for another twenty minutes. Considering how busy the bars were there didn't seem to be anyone else on this stretch of river. It did cross my mind that there could be bandits up there watching me.

I stood in the queue waiting to hand my tube and waterproof diving bag back to reclaim my four Dollar deposit. I looked down the line of drunken bodies. It didn't seem worth the wait for such a little amount, but I waited anyway. I could see taxi's waiting at the top of the hill. Two men started arguing over tubes a few yards in front of me. One claimed the other had stolen his when he went to the toilet. They were both very drunk. One too many buckets of alcohol each. I smoked a cigarette and watched as they started pushing each other. It's funny how when men have had too much to drink the paltry sum of four Dollars seems worth beating each other over. I wondered what they did for a living in the real world and whether either of them would even get out of bed for such an amount. Two policemen were laughing and pointing to the one they thought would have the better outcome of this drunken duel. A couple of minutes of chest bumping and swearing it was obvious to everyone unfortunate enough to be standing in the line that it wasn't going to get any more violent. I had bored enough of waiting in the sun and listening to their shit.

'Mate.' I shouted and started walking towards them. They were touching foreheads now. 'Since neither of you look likely to actually hit the other you can have mine.'

'What.'

'Take it. I'm bored of waiting and you two are starting to annoy everyone here, so take mine.' I handed him the inner tube and bag.

'Are you sure?'

I didn't answer and walked towards the taxi rank. A few people booed obviously wanting the show to continue. The policemen nodded their approval as I passed them. I had saved them having to do any work this afternoon and they could stay in the shade for a little while longer.

Charlotte had been right about this day. I hadn't enjoyed it. There were too many people and the whole thing seemed to be aimed at people who like busy nightclubs. I wasn't sure what I had expected and had only really liked wallowing on a rubber tube and drinking on my own. Maybe if there were a few bars where you could get off sit at a table and just enjoy a quiet beer, I could have got on board with it more. The relentless barrage of European dance music and pricks with aluminous paint smeared over their bodies despite it being broad daylight had made the day harder to bare, especially on my own. Charlie would have pinched my nose and told me to not be cynical. Everybody has the right to enjoy themselves she would have said. I instantly regretted burning her phone number.

CHAPTER 30.

'Dad. Can you hear me?'

'Ruben is that you? The lines awful.'

'I'm leaving Laos.'

'Love, it's Ruben. He's definitely pissed again. He's rambling on about something.'

I heard the phone change hands. 'Mum, can you hear me?'

'I can hear you fine darling it's that buffoon. Couldn't hear you if you stood next to him and screamed. Right, where the bloody hell are you and why haven't you called in best part of two months?'

'It's nice out here mum. I won't say I've relaxed more, but I'm definitely trying. I'm just about to head back into Thailand. I've met someone as well.'

'Bloody hell Ruben. Let's not go down there again. Tell me she's not one of those poor girls I've seen on TV?'

'Oh yeah. I went to see your uncles grave in Thailand. It was beautiful.'

'Wow, thank you Ruben. You're the only one who made it out there. Your grandad would have been happy.'

I started tearing up. 'Listen mum, I have to go. I need to be across the border in a little while to catch my train.'

'Ok dear. I'd put your dad on, but there isn't much point.'

'I love you mum. I'll call again soon. Not sure how much longer I'll be out here, money is running a little low.'

'Do you need me to send you some?'

'No, it's fine. Speak soon.' I heard her say love and I hung up wiping tears from my cheeks.

The bus journey from Vang Vieng had been pretty uneventful. The usual AK-47's and handguns on show to protect us from the Laos version of Jesse James and his crew. I had slept and drank in equal measures.

Crossing the bridge, I had an enormous feeling of wellbeing. Like I was coming home. I stopped halfway and peered down into the Mekong. It seemed strange that this would possibly be the last time I saw this great river. It felt an age since I had crossed it for the first time. While most tourists take the shuttle bus on offer from one border control to the next, I had decided to walk. I had a little time to kill before the train left Nong Khai train station and I knew it would be somewhere worth missing. Also, the idea of walking across the border had a certain romance to it. I poured some whiskey before making my way to the Thai side. Felt like the thing to do in the spur of the moment. Probably not great when I think back on it.

The train was nice. Fairly modern from the outside and had a good smell to it. I found my seat and after having my ticket checked twice by the same guard I was left alone. I had booked a second-class sleeper berth for the overnight to Bangkok and to be honest I was quite looking forward to it. Never having intentionally slept on a train before I had no idea what to expect. My seat faced towards the entrance, so I got to see everyone running around and searching for their carriage. A mother and her son sat on the adjacent side of the aisle to me. As soon as they sat down, he started acting up. I tried to concentrate on the book I was reading. I had found a copy of The Great Gatsby in the hostel in Vang Vieng and decided to give it a go. Halfway through and it was very good. This little shit opposite me wouldn't let up. You could tell his mother was trying, but he kept kicking her legs and throwing himself about. She looked at me in an apologetic fashion and said something in Thai.

'You speak English?' She gave me a blank stare. 'Children.' I raised my eyes. She didn't understand what I had said.

The kid stared at me like I had just tried to rape his poor mum in front of him and then went back to throwing his head back against the seat. I tried to ignore him and faced the window, but it had no effect. I could still see his reflection with that little face and shit haircut.

'Excuse me.' Same vacant look on her face that only a mother on the edge can give. 'Control your son, please.'

This was going to be a long night. I considered smothering him if he kept on. She said something to him in Thai and pointed at me.

'I understand English very well.' The boy said. 'Don't speak to my mother again.'

He couldn't have been older than eleven and here he was giving me orders. 'Does she speak any English?'

He leant across the aisle. 'Not a word. She is stupid.' He sneered at me.

I thought for a moment and held his arm. I smiled at his mum. 'Ok. Can you translate to her that if she doesn't control you and you ruin possibly the only journey, I'm likely to enjoy I will kill you in your sleep you spoilt little cunt.' I let go and smiled at both of them.

The colour drained from his face. I guess no one had ever spoken to him in that way before. I'm not proud of my actions and have never spoken to a child like that before or since, but sometimes they really get on your tits. He sat back in his chair. His mother asked him a question, but he waved it away. I'm sure I see him wipe a tear from his fat little face.

The train moved slowly out of the station and I rested the book on the table and watched as the sun cast shadows over the countryside. There were glasses on the table in front of me. I turned one over and filled it to the brim. Sipping the whiskey and letting it gently slide down my throat it warmed my insides. It wasn't the best whiskey, but it would do. There were definitely worse ways to travel. I closed my eyes and tried to remember the last time I hadn't been drunk or slightly intoxicated. When Charlotte left me, it had all gone to hell. I picked up Gatsby and tried to focus on the pages.

Around an hour into the trip the guard returned and presented me with a menu. I wasn't expecting dinner, so this was a nice surprise. I ordered the chicken and rice and a couple of Thai beers. As I waited for the food I wondered when we would be shown to the sleeping areas. I couldn't work out where on the train they were. I had walked at least half of the train to where I now sat and hadn't seen anything.

'Excuse me.' The guard had come back with the food and drinks. 'When do we move to the beds?' The boy opposite snorted and shook his head. I really hated him, and I don't think I had ever hated a child before.

'I'm sorry sir?'

'The beds, where are the beds? I booked a sleeping berth.'

'Later yes. First you eat. I come back for beds.' He placed the food trays neatly in front of me and slid the plastic cutlery next to them. Opening one of the cans of beer he poured half into the empty glass and left me to it. The service was outstanding. If this was second class, I regretted being too tight to upgrade for an extra few pounds to first.

I ate the chicken and rice and enjoyed the cold beer. It was dark outside and rolling through the countryside with only the occasional village light made it feel like one long giant tunnel all the way to Bangkok. The meal considering it was pre-made and reheated was one of the best I had eaten the whole time I had been in Asia. Chucking the knife and fork into the dish I picked up the glass and rested back, the seat was comfortable enough for me to consider just sleeping in that rather than trying to find the bed compartment. I read a few chapters and relaxed. The annoying little shit had fallen asleep and for the first time his mother seemed to enjoy the ride and was slowly drinking a glass of wine. Savouring every undisturbed mouthful. She didn't seem as worried by the lack of beds as I was.

'Sir, if you please, I will make your bed.'

Before me stood the guard and a young-looking helper. I had no idea what he could mean by make your bed. 'OK. Go on then.'

No one moved. I drank the last of the beer while they conversed in Thai. The mother caught my eye and made a stand-up motion with her hands. I slowly followed her gesture not knowing what was happening. The guard smiled politely and moved in to hand the glasses and empty dishes to the boy behind him who disposed of them in the blink of an eye. I stood to the side and watched as in a flurry of hands a few seconds the seats had been turned into a bed with the overhead compartments becoming a ceiling with lights and draw curtain. I was amazed once more and loved this country even more.

'That's marvellous.' I said. 'Where do I sit now though?'

'Bed is made for you sir.'

I looked at my watch. 'Mate it's fucking half eight.'

'Ok, thank you sir. Good night.'

He turned his back on me and preceded to convert the mother and son's side also into beds. Their side had a top bunk. I instantly forgot about the time and was slightly jealous that my side didn't have this elevated sleeping arrangement. I had genuinely never slept on a top bunk before.

The little boy dozed as they finished the makeover before being helped inside the curtain to the lower level. It amused me to think how upset he would be waking in the morning to realise he had missed out.

still learning her times. 'You miss bus no refund.'

I handed my passport over snatched up the room key and headed to the stairs. I reached the third floor and honestly stopped in horror. It was like a gulag or some other internment camp. Along each side of the corridor were green wooden doors. None of which appeared to be in good order. A child's shoulder would have made anyone of them give way. The lights finished the effect of shear depression. I considered asking for my money back and going to see Alan.

Reaching lucky number fifteen I pushed the door before trying the key. It opened easily. Inside can only be described as a cell. A double bed to the left with a TV precariously placed on a stand above the foot end. It was a bonus, but that was it. There wasn't room for anything else. The walls were a single sheet of plasterboard or something similar, the top few inches missing. I threw my bag on the bed "One night" I said out loud to no one in particular. Squeezing myself in to the bathroom I stood facing a hole in the building equal to at least double the size of my head. This was the window, ventilation and escape hatch rolled into one. It also looked onto someone's balcony. An old man smiled at me and waved. I waved back. The shower was another garden hose over the toilet which saves a lot of time in the mornings. I couldn't face anymore so went to find somewhere to eat and drink.

CHAPTER 32.

Watching the other travellers in the restaurant I couldn't understand why they had come all this way. They lounged around each other's tables talking of where they intended to go next and the plans they had. That was it. Everyone seemed intent on congregating in the same places. They were carbon copies of each other. No one willing to take a chance and go it alone. Safety in numbers. The last proper traveller I had met was Freja.

The longer I sat there watching them the more annoyed I became. It could have been because they reminded me that I was still like them in some ways. The need to be loved and have a sense of belonging had hindered me from the day I was born. I stewed for hours sneering at their ideas and chat. "Let's go to the islands" they would say. "The parties down there are great". I laughed at their need to move in herds. I wanted to scream at them to try something new. Something different. See who they would meet at the next destination. That should be why you're all here not to simply transport the parties of Europe to more tropical climes. But then why was I here? I had done nothing exceptional while here. I was no better than the idiot in the tank top shouting about climbing some fucking hill no one cared about. Who was I to lecture these people.

I drank until I could barely stand. My mind was faltering I knew that much. My thoughts were incoherent and muddled. At one point I thought Charlie had sat next to me. Dressed as she had the last time, we had had breakfast together. Her t-shirt and my pants. I still loved her. I would always love her. I drooled and cried. The other guests laughed and pointed. It was becoming harder to care.

Waking in my room it was as dark outside as it was in this cell. My neighbour had crashed through his door a couple of minutes previously. I could hear the rustling of foil and a lighter flicking on trying to spark. The noxious smell of heroin filled both of our rooms. There were two voices. The first clearly an American man. The second was Thai, this one sounded a mix of male and female. I laughed to myself wondering whether he knew he was with a ladyboy. He probably didn't care so good luck to the both of them. I felt my shorts. I had pissed myself and had no idea how I had gotten back to my room. I slept again.

I was shaken awake. Not by someone in my room, but by the wall moving from next door fucking the night away. I had rolled over at some point and my face was pressed against the wall no more than a few centimetres from another man or men's penis's. I found my cigarettes and lit one. It was still dark. I couldn't see my watch. The noise stopped after a few minutes. No climax achieved. I could hear someone moving around trying to find something. It aggravated me that I couldn't see. One ear against the thin wall I blew smoke up towards the gap above.

'Hey. Are you fucking listening? You fucking pervert.'

I held my breath for a moment. This American was obviously out of his mind on gear.

'You fucking creep.' He banged the wall.

'Mate, you haven't exactly given me much of a choice. How much longer you going to be? I have a bus to catch in the morning.'

Nothing for a few seconds. I listened.

'Shit, sorry buddy. You know how it can get.' He chuckled which made me feel a little sick. 'Where you heading?'

'Koh Chang.'

'Beautiful place.'

'I've heard.'

'We'll try to keep it down for you buddy, but I can't guarantee anything. These graceful creatures really get my blood pumping. You know?'

'Not really no, but thanks.' I slid the butt into the empty bottle by my side, rolled over and closed my eyes.

'Hey buddy...'

'Yeah?'

'You wanna share some smack?'

'Nope.'

CHAPTER 33.

'Where you want to go?'

'Lonely Beach.'

'Lonely Beach?'

'Lonely Beach.'

'Wait for some more then leave.'

I rested on the back step of the taxi come bus. They waited until people had to stand on the back before setting off around the island. It made sense even if it could take half an hour to leave the port. Not that I minded. I was on a beautiful island in the middle of the Gulf of Thailand with the sun on my face and a packet of cigarettes in my pocket.

The boat across hadn't been too bad. I had vomited a few times over the side much to the delight of a group of young South Africans. A mixture of hangover and sea sickness. I knew Charlotte would either be here or on her way. The only problem was I didn't know if I cared too much. I didn't feel about her the way I had first thought. If I did, I wouldn't be constantly dreaming of Charlie. My mind was a mess.

As soon as we arrived at the beach I relaxed. It was stunning. Sitting on my bag on the sand I watched the sea gently roll up the shore then slowly recede again. The water wasn't even turquoise to call it that would be a disservice it was clear. As simple as that. I walked down and let the warm waters cover my feet. Up and down the beach young and almost young people sat around smoking and sunbathing. A little further down I watched a very pretty girl on a swing. She was in a world of her own. Her boyfriend took photos of her as she too watched the sea. This was paradise for many of them.

I checked into the beach huts with the biggest restaurant. It wasn't a conscious decision it had simply been the first one on the beach I had come across. My hut was around three rows back from the sea. I didn't want to be right on the beach. Especially after what had happened the other year. Although I don't think an extra forty foot would save you, but certainly gave the illusion that it would.

Sitting down in the restaurant I ordered a couple of beers and a noodle soup. Looking at everyone else I noticed lots of them had cameras. Some even had the huge lenses that professional journalists used attached. I happily smoked a cigarette while drinking my beer. The sun had started setting when I had first sat down. The restaurant was packed with everyone laying back drinking and chatting between tables. All facing the same direction there was a real sense of community here. It felt as though everyone knew each other. I was the odd one out who needed to earn their place in the group.

The sun finally caught up with everybody else's anticipation and began to set fully behind the small out crop island at the far end of the beach. The world stopped for a brief moment, the waves ceased their relentless drive, and the birds gave up their incessant chirping. As the sun disappeared behind the horizon people began clapping and cheering. Their flashes could have induced an epileptic seizure. It was beautiful. Possibly one of the most beautiful things I had ever seen, but the applause was a bit much.

CHAPTER 34.

I hadn't slept well. The bed was comfortable enough, but there was a section of board missing in the roof space. Every time the wind blew it made a whistling noise that woke me. I was going to ask to be moved until I noticed that all the huts were the same. I'd try to see where Charlotte was staying before moving on.

The restaurant was busy again. There were the same faces as the night before sitting in the same places. I ordered a coke and sat near the front overlooking the beach. I listened in to the next table discussing feeding monkeys somewhere.

'Excuse me.' I wanted to know where the monkeys were. 'Excuse me.'

'Yes.'

'I hope you don't mind the intrusion, but where are the monkeys?'

They looked at me like I was odd. I Suppose I was. I still hadn't shaved so must have looked like a tramp or a terrorist.

'Up on the main road, opposite the 7/11.'

'Oh, right. What type of food do you feed them?'

'The shop sells it.'

'Ok, cool. Thank you. I'm Ruben by the way.'

'Ok.' They didn't offer up their own names and went back to their conversation. This time a little quieter.

I put a straw in my coke and sucked half down in one go.

People were going for a morning swim. I thought about joining them, but that's about as far as it went. Someone caught my attention out of the corner of my eye. Charlotte looked amazing. Her browned body was more beautiful than I could have ever imagined. She padded up the sand and I stood raising my hand ready to wave and call her name. There was someone else waiting for her, towel in hand.

Taller than me and definitely more muscular. He had great hair that had obviously been professionally curated before this trip. He wrapped his huge arms around her, and she giggled. I sat back down. The world stopped once more. It had only been a week or so. I couldn't quite place the time since I had last seen her, but it surely wasn't that long. Who was this intruder. Was he an intruder at all since I wasn't sure if I at all bothered about seeing her again. Was I now the intruder. I watched them for over an hour. Skulking in the shadows. She was happy. Not once did she look towards the entrance to the beach to see if I had arrived for our great romantic rekindling. They kissed as we had kissed back in Luang Prabang on those long afternoons by the Mekong.

I needed to get away. There was no point speaking to Charlotte. She had made a decision to replace me with a better alternative and how could I blame her. She was a young gorgeous, intelligent woman and deserved someone who didn't hate themselves and the world around them. I went to find a travel agent to get me the fuck out of here.

'Hi. Can you change international airline tickets?'

'Of course.'

'Good.' I produced my homeward bound pass.

The man studied the piece of paper. 'You want to change date or destination?'

I sat back in the chair. 'I can change the destination?'

'You can whatever you like for fee.'

I stared at him for a few seconds.

'So, what to change?' The man held the phone limply in his hand.

'Bring it forward to two days' time.'

'Destination? Still London or somewhere new? Possibility endless.' He started dialling.

'Edinburgh.'

CHAPTER 35.

Sitting on the shoreline I watched as the sun lose its fight once more. I turned back to the restaurant as the other travellers clapped and cheered as they had possibly done every night since arriving and witnessing someone else doing the same. I realised I had nothing in common with these people. I didn't hate them. Why would I. They were simply enjoying the best moments of their lives. Sucking in every last drop of the experience. But that just wasn't me. I was too cynical. Too self-loathing.

The warm sea gently covered my feet. It was relaxing and comforting. The sea has a natural draw to humans. It's there buried deep in our sub-conscious. Finishing a half bottle of whiskey, I looked around at the discarded cigarette butts and empty bottles that surrounded me. It was the biggest achievement in life.

I slowly pushed myself up and opened the last bottle of whiskey. I had treated myself to a bottle of Jameson. Not that easy to get out here. I wondered if going to find Charlie was a mistake. How the fuck would I find her anyway. She could have been lying and not even be in Scotland at all. I lit up. The sun had finally set and the lights from the restaurant now lit the beach almost all the way down to my hiding place. This was it for me. Drinking, smoking, and blaming the world.

'I'm going for a swim.' I screamed to no one. The music from the different beach side bars drowned me out anyway. I walked in and lay back in the almost still water. I held my ears just below the surface so I could only hear my heartbeat. I ducked my head backwards fully under this time. The sea rushed into my nose and stung the back of my throat, but it didn't bother me. I did it again and again trying to feel something. The voices came quietly at first, whispering in the background as they always did. I held my head under longer to silence them and their whisper became louder. Suddenly I couldn't hear my heartbeat anymore and they stopped their incessant noise. Everything stopped. My entire anxiety driven life gave way to peace. I didn't belong here, I never had. I had no thought for anyone else in this moment. It may be selfish, but I was free. Some of us struggle through this life. It's not our fault it is just who we are and as much as we try it just isn't going to work out. The only thing that really sets us apart from the rest of humanity is that we are never meant to make to the end. We aren't supposed to grow old and have the family home. I'm not making excuses or asking for forgiveness I'm only saying don't blame us for making the ultimate choice. It's a relief we can't quite explain.

The End.

Printed in Great Britain
by Amazon

18991231R00089